FULL-BLOODED FANTASY

8 Spellbinding Tales in Which Anything Is Possible

♦ **SELECTIONS FROM** ♦

The Spiderwick Chronicles,
Pendragon,
and more

Simon & Schuster Children's Publishing
New York ♦ London ♦ Toronto ♦ Sydney

Simon & Schuster Children's Publishing Division ✦ 1230 Avenue of the Americas, New York, NY 10020 ✦ *The Sea of Trolls* copyright © 2004 by Nancy Farmer ✦ *The Water Mirror* copyright © 2001 by Kai Meyer ✦ *Spiderwick Chronicles: The Field Guide* copyright © 2003 by Tony DiTerlizzi and Holly Black ✦ *The Conch Bearer* copyright © 2005 by Chitra Banerjee Divakaruni ✦ *The Farsala Trilogy: Fall of a Kingdom* copyright © 2003 by Hilari Bell ✦ *Pendragon #6: The Rivers of Zadaa* copyright © 2005 by D. J. MacHale ✦ *Clemency Pogue* copyright © 2005 by JT Perry ✦ *May Bird and the Ever After* text copyright © 2005 by Jodi Lynn Anderson; illustrations copyright © 2005 by Leonid Gore

This book contains excerpts from books previously or soon to be published individually by Simon & Schuster Children's Publishing Division.

Manufactured in the United States of America
First Aladdin Paperbacks edition May 2005
10 9 8 7 6 5 4 3 2 1
ISBN-13: 978-0-689-04867-8
ISBN-10: 0-689-04867-X

SELECTIONS FROM

The Sea of Trolls
by Nancy Farmer

DARK REFLECTIONS
Book One: The Water Mirror
by Kai Meyer

May Bird and the Ever After
by Jodi Lynn Anderson

THE SPIDERWICK CHRONICLES
#1: The Field Guide
By Tony DiTerlizzi and Holly Black

Clemency Pogue: Fairy Killer
by JT Petty
illustrated by Will Davis

The Conch Bearer
By Chitra Banerjee Divakaruni

THE FARSALA TRILOGY BOOK 1
Fall of a Kingdom
by Hilari Bell

PENDRAGON
Book Six: The Rivers of Zadaa
by D. J. MacHale

FROM SIMON & SCHUSTER CHILDREN'S PUBLISHING

THE SEA OF TROLLS

by NANCY FARMER

THREE-TIME NEWBERY HONOR AUTHOR

NANCY FARMER

THE SEA of TROLLS

The year is A.D. 793. Jack and his little sister, Lucy, are enslaved by Olaf One-Brow and his fierce young shipmate, Thorgil. With a crow named Bold Heart for company, they are swept up into an adventure that will not be forgotten. This *New York Times* bestseller from award-winning author Nancy Farmer tells one boy's story of outwitting all expectations.

NANCY FARMER has written three Newbery Honor Books: *The Ear the Eye and the Arm*; *A Girl Named Disaster*; and *The House of the Scorpion*, which in 2002 also won the National Book Award. Other books include *Do You Know Me*, *The Warm Place*, and three picture books for young children. She grew up on the Arizona-Mexico border, and now lives with her family in Menlo Park, California.

Visit www.SimonSaysKids.com for more on *The Sea of Trolls*, including a downloadable screensaver, an interview with Nancy Farmer, and a reading group guide.

A Richard Jackson Book
Atheneum Books for Young Readers
New York ✦ London ✦ Toronto ✦ Sydney

Chapter Ten

OLAF ONE-BROW

Jack sat in a hollow near the Roman road. He was surrounded by bracken like a rabbit hiding from a fox. No one would be able to see him, but Jack intended to be even more invisible. He breathed in the green odors of earth and fern. He felt with his mind the damp roots of trees. *Come forth,* he called. *Come forth to me. Cloak the air with your gray presences. Bring sea and sky together.*

He felt, rather than saw, the curling mist. Sunlight muted to pearl white, to dove feather and dusk. Dampness flowed into his lungs. Water gathered on ferns. Round drops paused on the tips of leaves and fell, sending pale threads over moss. The air sighed and rustled with it.

He had never been so deep in the life force. He swam through it like a minnow, like a woodland creature with no more thought than to *be*. It was enough. It was more than enough. The glory and wonder of it swept him on.

"Jack . . . Jack . . ."

The voice reached him from a great distance. He turned from it, unwilling to become human again.

"Jack . . . oh, please! I'm so cold and scared!"

He came to his senses. For a moment he was filled with unreasoning anger. How dare anyone disturb him!

He heard gulping, hiccuping cries that cut him to the heart. It was Lucy! She was nearby but hidden by a fog so thick and heavy, it frightened even Jack. He'd really outdone himself this time. "Lucy, I'm here," he called.

"Where's 'here'? It's so dark and awful. I know there's monsters." She began to sob.

"Don't move, Lucy. Just keep talking so I can find you."

"When I went outside, it was sunny. You were *supposed* to be in the garden. Father said you were in the garden, but you *weren't*." Some of Lucy's fear was replaced by indignation.

Jack tripped over a rock and scratched himself on a branch.

"I saw you from far away," said Lucy. "You were walking fast. I wanted to call, but I didn't want Mother to know I was outside. She's been so mean to me today. She wouldn't let me play outside or anything."

Jack thought Mother was out of her mind with worry. She knew the danger they were in. So did Father, but he chose to ignore it.

"I walked to the Roman road, but you were gone. You went off and left me. Bad Jack! Then the fog came in really fast. It got dark and I got scared. Have you been doing magic? Father says wizards do magic and then they go to Hell. Are you going to Hell?"

"I couldn't even find it in this fog," muttered Jack. He felt the edge of the road with his feet. A moment later he saw Lucy crouched on the stones. He touched her arm, and she screamed. "It's me," he said, fending off her blows.

"Why did you sneak up on me like that?" she wailed.

"I wasn't sneaking—oh, never mind. Listen, I've got a very important job to do, and I need you to be quiet."

"I'm always quiet. I can keep my mouth shut for hours. Father says I'm like a dear little mouse. He said I was changed into a mouse by a bad fairy when I lived in the palace, but a good fairy changed me back."

"How about being quiet now?" Jack said. It seemed to him the air was beginning to move. Perhaps a sea wind had sprung up.

"It's a good story. I can tell it really well. Father says I know as many words as a ten-year-old."

"Shh!" Jack pulled her down into the bracken.

"I'm getting wet," cried Lucy.

"Be quiet. Someone's coming along the road," Jack whispered. "Maybe a monster," he added. Lucy clung to him and made no more complaints about wetness. In the distance they heard voices. They were too far to distinguish words, but something about the sound made Jack's hair prickle on the back of his neck. Then, shockingly, someone blew a hunting horn nearby.

Lucy tried to dive under Jack's shirt. He held her close, feeling her tremble and himself tremble. Far away another horn answered.

"*Hvað er Þetta?*" someone said so close that Jack almost yelled. He heard more voices—four or five. The fog was definitely thinning. He could see shapes on the road, shaggy beings who walked with a heavy tread. He heard the clank of swords.

Come forth. Come forth to me. Cloak the air with your gray presences, he called to the life force, but his concentration was broken. Terror threatened to overwhelm him. These were the wolf-headed men. They were real. They were on the way to the village.

"Are those knights?" whispered Lucy.

"No. Be quiet." Even without fog, Jack thought they would be well hidden in the bracken. They could escape. But what of Father and Mother? Or the Bard?

"I think they're knights," Lucy said.

"They're monsters. Be quiet."

"*Hvað?*" said one of the men on the road. He strode to the edge and peered out over the bracken.

"*Ekkert. Þetta er bara kanína,*" said another.

The words were almost like Saxon, Jack's own tongue. He'd heard a few other languages in his life, from people who passed through at village fairs. He'd heard Welsh, Erse, Pictish, and of course Latin, but he could speak none of them. They were nothing like his own speech. This was. He was almost certain the first man had said *What?* and the second had replied *Nothing. It's only a rabbit.*

Lucy wriggled beside him, and he tightened his hold on her. The warriors above were growing ever more clear. They were cloaked in sheepskins and wore leather caps over their long, pale hair. Swords and axes hung from their belts. One was only a boy.

For a long moment the men conferred, and then, miraculously, they turned back the way they had come. They would miss the village! Jack hugged Lucy. "They're going," she whispered.

"Shh," said Jack. The boy had turned and was once again scanning the bracken.

"*Komdu,* Thorgil," called one of the men.

"They're the knights come to take me to my castle," Lucy cried out suddenly. "Here I am! Here!"

The boy on the road shouted, "*Þarna er kanínan!*" He leaped into the bracken, knife in hand, and grabbed Lucy. Jack tried to knock him down, but the boy yanked her up by the hair and held the knife to her throat. By now the men were running back.

Jack had one instant—only one—in which he could have fled, leaving Lucy behind in the clutches of the berserkers. He couldn't do it. She was so little and helpless. He was her brother. He had no hope of defeating such a band of warriors, but he could stay with her, little though that might accomplish. At least they would die together.

In the next instant a huge man with one bushy eyebrow extending across his forehead fell on Jack like a tree and knocked him senseless.

❖❖❖

The ground was moving. It tossed him up first and then slid him down in a nauseating roll. Jack gulped for air, got foul-tasting water instead, and then he did vomit. He crouched on hands and knees. He had been lying facedown in a filthy pool, and his whole body was wet and cold. The ground heaved again.

"*Þrællinn er vaknaður,*" someone said.

Jack's head throbbed. He looked down to see a

drop of blood plop into the disgusting pool. He felt his hair. It was matted and sticky. How had that happened?

"Hei þræll! Þú hefur svolitið kettlingaklór þarna." There was crude laughter, and several other voices joined in.

Jack struggled to understand. They were speaking something like Saxon, but the accent was so barbaric, he could make out only one word in three. Was *þræll* their word for *thrall*? If so—Jack had to think hard—it meant "servant" or possibly "slave." That didn't sound good. *Kettlingur*, which was close to *kettlingaklór*, meant "kitten." What did kittens have to do with him?

Jack looked up—his head hurt so much, he was afraid to move quickly. The ground pitched again, and he saw, beyond a wooden railing, a vast expanse of gray water. He looked to the other side. More water.

He was on a ship! Jack had been in little coracles close to shore. He used them to reach small islands at low tide, to gather seagull eggs and whelks. He never went far. Now he saw no islands, only a heaving gray sea with a pitiless gray sky above. He moaned and ducked his head to shut out the ter-rible sight.

"*Skræfan þín.*"

Skrafan thin. Jack easily translated that into his own language. It was a favorite insult thrown back and forth between the village boys: "scaredy-pants." Well, he *was* scared. Who wouldn't be? He was adrift on the open sea with no memory of how he got there.

He turned to get a look at who was talking and flinched. It was a *giant.* Maybe not a true giant—they were supposed to have hands big enough to pick up an ox. But this creature was certainly taller than any man Jack had seen. He had blond braids hanging past his shoulders, a massive beard covering his chest, and one bushy eyebrow extending all the way across his face.

Now the boy remembered. In that fragment of time between seeing Lucy with a knife at her throat and the utter darkness that followed, there was an instant where a huge one-browed man had hurled himself at Jack. This was he! This was a berserker in the flesh, every bit as dreadful as the stories said. Beyond him Jack saw other men pulling on oars. They were smaller than the giant but just as evil-looking.

Lucy! What had happened to her? Had they—? It was unthinkable! But men who could slaughter the gentle monks would think nothing of killing a girl. Jack closed his eyes. He had failed to save the one person he was bound to protect. His fragile little sister had been tossed aside as if she were of no more importance than a mouse.

He found that having his eyes closed made him even more seasick.

Jack pulled himself up and staggered to the rail. It would take only a small effort to throw himself over the side. Why not? What did he have to live for? Lucy was dead, perhaps even his parents. He didn't know what had happened while he was unconscious. His future was bleak. The berserkers would probably kill him in some entertaining way. They might even *eat* him.

Jack felt dizzy with pain and despair. He'd failed everyone, even the Bard. If the old man hadn't given him the rune of protection, he might have withstood the Nightmare.

Jack felt at his neck. There it was, invisible but still warm to the touch. What a laugh! It saved his life for what? He was a miserable failure who let berserkers kill his sister. He let the Nightmare steal the Bard's wits. The poor old man would wander until he found the Valley of Lunatics. At least there he'd make friends.

Jack's mouth quirked. What was *wrong* with him? He had nothing to smile about. Yet the thought of the Bard having a party in the Valley of Lunatics—all of them saying "wudduh" and "gaaw" and nodding wisely—well, it was *kind* of funny. *No, it's not,* Jack told himself sternly.

Yes, it is, said his mouth, insisting on quirking up.

He felt warmth spreading from the hidden rune. It filled him with a distant hope. After all, he didn't know that his parents were dead. The Bard might recover. Life was precious and not to be thrown away heedlessly.

At that moment Jack looked down the length of the boat and saw the boy who'd killed Lucy. Jack lurched forward, but he saw he wouldn't get past the men. They sat squarely in the middle, each one hauling on a pair of oars. The giant sat in front on a wooden chest.

"*Hvert ertu að fara?*" said the giant.

Where are you going? Jack translated.

"To kill that boy," he said, pointing.

For a moment the giant appeared to be working it out. Then his eyes opened wide. "*Að drepa þetta brjóstabarn. Ha! Ha! Ha! Ha!*"

"*Ég er ekki brjóstabarn!*" came the outraged voice of the boy.

"*Jú, það ertu!*"

The men all seemed to find this extremely funny. They roared and hooted. The boy protested in his higher, shriller voice.

"*Það er gott,*" said the giant, wiping tears from his eyes. He moved his tree-trunk-size legs to one side and signaled the other men to do likewise. "*Að drepa þetta brjóstabarn. Ha! Ha! Ha! Ha!*"

What kind of people were these? thought Jack. They knew he wanted to commit murder, and they liked it! He didn't understand the word *brjóstabarn*, but *drepa* most definitely meant "kill." He pushed his way past the berserkers, stepping over legs and under elbows. He didn't know what he was going to do when he got back there.

He came out from under the last smelly, sheepskin-clad arm and tripped over Lucy. She was crouched in the dirty water at the bottom of the boat. "It's about time," she sniffled. "I've been suffering most horribly, and all you did was sleep."

"You're alive! Oh, thank Heaven!" He hugged his little sister, who at once burst into tears.

"I've been trying to tell these knights to take me to the castle," she sobbed.

"They aren't knights," Jack said, unsure of how much to tell Lucy.

"You can say that again! They smell like hogs and bark like dogs. And they laugh at me. Tell them to take us home right now."

"I don't think they'll obey me," said Jack.

"*Hei þræll! Því drepurðu ekki þetta brjóstabarn?*"

"He's asking why you don't kill me," said the boy in perfect Saxon. "If you try, I'll cut your head off." He continued plying his oar, which was different from the others. It hung from a kind of hinge and went straight down into the water.

"You're the *brjóstabarn*?" Jack said.

For answer, the boy kicked Jack in the stomach and followed up with another blow to the head. "You're a dirty thrall. I can kill you whenever I want."

The blow opened up the cut on Jack's head. He wanted to fight back, but he was too weak. All he could manage was to hold his stomach and try to keep from vomiting.

"You monster!" shrieked Lucy. "You—you *brjóstabarn!*" She scrambled under the forest of arms and legs to the giant and climbed onto his lap by pulling on his braids.

"No . . . no . . . ," moaned Jack. He expected the giant to hurl Lucy into the sea.

"You've got to do something!" Lucy was screaming. "You're my knights, and you're supposed to be taking me to my castle. Get off that box and beat that *brjóstabarn!*"

Instead of getting angry, the giant gave another of his barking laughs. He put Lucy down and made his way to the stern of the boat. It swayed sickeningly under his weight. *"Hann er þrællinn minn, Thorgil,"* he said, slapping the boy so hard, his head snapped back. *"Þú mátt ekki drepa hann."* Then he trudged back to his box.

Thorgil ground his teeth, but he didn't utter a sound. He glared at Jack with a hatred so intense, Jack could almost feel it. Meanwhile, Lucy had returned. She squatted in the dirty water and patted Jack's arm. "I'll protect you," she said. "After all, I'm a princess."

Gradually, the bleeding stopped, and Jack was able to recover from the vicious blow to his stomach. He couldn't think of a thing to do, other than stay alive for Lucy's sake. She had no idea of their extreme danger. To her, this was merely an uncomfortable adventure.

After a long while Thorgil turned to Jack and once again spoke in perfect Saxon. "I will not kill you because you belong to Olaf One-Brow. It is his privilege to do so. However, the girl is my thrall." He smiled coldly. "I will kill her whenever I wish, if you displease me." And he turned again to ply his single oar.

Chapter Eleven

THE SHIELD MAIDEN

They traveled all day, with breaks to let the oarsmen rest. The sky remained gray, but the clouds lifted enough for Jack to see land far to the left. At one point they passed an island that trailed plumes of smoke. Was that the Holy Isle? It was too hazy to tell.

At one point the rowers halted, and Olaf One-Brow passed out smoked fish, cheese, and a kind of flatbread Jack had never seen before. He thought it delicious until he realized it had been stolen from some poor village. Olaf found a pot of honey and smeared it on the bread for Lucy. No one else got this treat.

"*Litla valkyrja,*" the giant rumbled, tousling Lucy's hair.

"Princess," corrected Lucy. They smiled at each other.

"Pest," said the boy at the oar.

Jack studied him. Thorgil was handsome, in a sullen way. His eyes were blue, and his hair would have been as golden as Lucy's if it hadn't been so dirty. The berserkers were all filthy, Jack realized. Their boots smelled like carrion, and their sheepskins reeked of sweat. Lucy, in her sky blue dress, looked like a flower dropped into a pigsty.

What was he to do about her? Jack might try swimming to shore by himself, but he couldn't leave her behind. Olaf One-Brow might possibly be talked into setting her free, but Lucy didn't belong to him. The berserkers set great store by ownership. Once Thorgil had pinched her, to see Jack's reaction, and Olaf had done nothing about it.

They slid north on the gray ocean until the sun broke out in late afternoon. It hovered, red and swollen, over the horizon as they turned toward land. Jack saw a dense forest and fires along the shore. Two other boats had been drawn up. Shouts greeted their arrival.

Altogether the warriors numbered about forty men and seven boys. The ones on shore were showing off the booty they had taken—embroidered shawls, necklaces, even pairs of dainty ladies' shoes draped about their necks like trophies. They pranced around, guffawing and pointing at one another. Other loot was displayed on the sand: metalwork, pottery, spoons, swags of richly colored cloth, and a jeweled cross that might have come from the Holy Isle. Huddled next to the forest were the captives, with their legs hobbled.

Jack was hustled to this group, but Lucy was presented like a rare prize to the assembled warriors. Olaf lifted her over his head and boomed *"Litla valkyrja!"*

before he put her down. Everyone admired her. Lucy bowed. They bowed back. She clapped her hands and they laughed. She was caught up in her princess fantasy, but Jack was desperately worried about the berserkers' true motives.

"She's a little charmer, isn't she?" a woman said. She was thin, her eyes full of grief. "I had a daughter. She wasn't as beautiful as your sister." She fell silent, and Jack thought he knew what had happened. The woman's daughter had not been pretty enough to keep.

"The girl's a slave like the rest of us," said a man in a torn monk's robe. "They'll raise her like a prize pig and then sell her."

"At least she's alive," Jack said.

"Sometimes death is better."

"No, it isn't."

The monk laughed harshly. "Hark at him! The child presumes to lecture his elders. Listen, boy. Long life is but a chance to commit more sins. The longer you live, the more Satan whispers in your ear. Your soul grows so heavy, it gets dragged down to Hell. It's better to die young, preferably right after baptism, and be taken into Heaven."

"My daughter is in Heaven," said the sad-eyed woman.

"Yes, well, you don't know that," the monk said. "Even quite small children are capable of evil."

"I *know* she is," the woman said fiercely.

"And I believe you," said Jack. "I think it depends on whether someone means to be bad. My sister Lucy can drive you crazy, but she hasn't an evil bone in her body."

"Man is born corrupt," the monk said in a hollow voice. Jack made no answer. That was the sort of thing Father said all the time.

The warriors gorged themselves on roast meat until their bellies bulged and their beards shone with grease. They drank mead until they fell over. Fights broke out.

More than one man went to bed with a cut lip or a bloody nose, but it seemed to be in good fun. Jack noticed, however, that some did not take part.

Olaf One-Brow's group camped by themselves. No one playfully punched them or threw sand in their hair. No one uttered a catcall in their direction. It seemed that Olaf's men were too important to indulge in horseplay.

The exception was Thorgil. Another lad with chopped-off hair ran past the group and threw a pebble at the boy. Thorgil sprang to his feet with a shout and took off after the offender. Round and round they went until Thorgil caught up with his tormentor.

"*Hættu!*" cried the short-haired lad.

"*Aldrei! Nei!*" shouted Thorgil.

The others danced around, singing, "*Dreptu hann! Dreptu hann!*"

"They're saying, 'Kill him! Kill him!'" the monk said quietly.

"You know their language?" said Jack. Thorgil was getting the best of the fight because he was so much more frenzied.

"Oh, yes. I have had occasion to preach to these . . . animals."

By now the short-haired lad was trying to escape, but Thorgil pulled him back and proceeded to pound and kick him in a sickening way. The cries of the watchers changed to *"Nóg! Hættu!"*

"They're saying, 'Enough! Stop!' But she won't," said the monk.

"She?" Jack was startled from his fascination with the fight. It was getting nasty, with Thorgil pulling the boy's head back in an attempt to break his neck.

"Oh, yes. That's a girl."

"Nóg," growled Olaf One-Brow, plucking Thorgil from the fray as easily as picking up a kitten. The short-haired boy scuttled off on hands and knees. The others scattered.

"I'm surprised," said the monk. "Olaf usually lets a fight go through to the end." The giant lumbered back across the sand with Thorgil tucked firmly under his arm.

"How can that be a girl?" said Jack. He'd known some bad-tempered girls in the village, but none of them would have thrown themselves into such a vicious fight. None of the boys, either, for that matter.

"She's a shield maiden," said the monk. "A little abomination who will certainly toast her heels in Hell for all eternity. She's trying to make the grade with Olaf, so she's twice as likely to pick fights as his men. And they're no slouches." The monk stared long and hard at the group. By now most of the warriors had collapsed on the sand in a drunken stupor. Only Olaf's men spread cloths and lay down properly.

They formed a square as though, even in sleep, they were in military formation. In the middle lay Thorgil. Next to her, on a blanket, was Lucy. She had a real pillow and a richly embroidered cover that might have been taken from a church altar.

"What's a *brjóstabarn*?" said Jack.

"What a strange question," said the monk.

"It's what Olaf called Thorgil."

"Ah." The monk nodded in somber understanding. "It means 'suckling baby.' He's calling Thorgil that to make her angry. Making people angry is a favorite pastime of the Northmen."

"And what is a—" Jack had to stop to recall the word. "—a *kettlingaklór*?"

The monk laughed bitterly. "It means 'kitten scratch.' It's what these people call a blow that knocks you flat. I gather you had one."

"Yes," said Jack.

"You seem no worse for it. Trust me, you don't want to find out what a really big cat scratch feels like."

With that, the monk withdrew into his own thoughts and refused to talk. Jack watched the flickering fires, the sprawled warriors, and the neat square where Olaf and his people lay.

The captives were guarded by three men, who had not been allowed to drink. Escape was impossible. Besides, Jack thought as he stretched out on the cold, damp ground, he couldn't leave without Lucy. And there was no way he was going to rescue her from that ominous square of Olaf's men.

❖❖❖

They camped on the beach for several days. Boats went out and returned with booty. Finally, when the warriors had amassed as much as they could carry, the whole group sailed north.

It was extremely uncomfortable. Jack and the other captives were packed like trussed-up chickens. They lay faceup, able to see only the sky and to feel the cold water sloshing under their backs. The boats leaked continuously. Captives were freed in shifts to bail them out. When it was Jack's turn, he was horrified to see how near the sea came to spilling inside. The boat was so heavily laden, one more roll of cloth could send them to the bottom.

That's a girl, he thought, eyeing Thorgil. He now understood that her oar was a rudder used to steer the boat. Plying a real oar would have been beyond her strength. Jack tried to imagine her in a dress and couldn't. She was too brutish. When the men tossed insults back and forth, she outdid them in malice. When they spat and farted, she joined in.

Altogether she was the most disgusting creature—male or female—Jack had ever seen. He had always to come between her and Lucy, for Thorgil's greatest joy was to cause pain. She never—quite—drew blood, but Lucy's arms were covered with bruises from pinches.

Jack wondered at the little girl's ability to keep up her spirits. Surely by now she knew she wasn't headed for a castle. At the very least she must miss Mother and Father. Yet Lucy picked herself up after every pinch, wiped her eyes, and found Olaf. She ordered him around like a favorite hound, and if the giant didn't actually obey her, Lucy pretended he did. It was curious and disturbing at the same time.

Olaf wasn't a safe companion. He dealt out punishment with a quick hand, breaking teeth or cracking a rib according to his mood. Seeing Lucy with the monster made Jack sick. But there was nothing he could do about it.

On the third day a storm rose. The boat rolled frighteningly and waves splashed over the side. All the captives bailed furiously while the oarsmen struggled to reach shore. The sad-eyed woman collapsed. She hadn't been strong to begin with. Olaf dragged her up, and with a swift movement that made Jack cry out, he cut her throat and threw her over the side.

Jack and the others were frozen for one long moment. Then they redoubled their efforts before Olaf turned his attention to them. Even so, the shore remained agonizingly distant. The oarsmen were pushed back by the wind and lost two strokes of progress for every three they made. Thorgil clung grimly to her rudder. The sea attempted to snatch it out of her control, but she ground her teeth and fought back.

"May angels carry you to your daughter's side," whispered the monk as he toiled. "May your time in purgatory be short."

He was praying for the poor, murdered woman. Tears rolled down Jack's face, mixed with rain. He didn't even know her name, and already her face was blurred in his memory. *May the life force hold you in the hollow of its hand,* Jack thought, repeating words he had learned from the Bard. *May you return with the sun and be born anew into the world.*

It wasn't a prayer Father would have liked. He would have knocked Jack six ways to Sunday for saying it. But Jack thought it right and sensible to call on two religions, in case one failed.

Lucy was packed between rolls of fur and cloth. Jack could hear her crying over the storm, which was so intense now, he couldn't see the stern of the boat. He tried not to think about the poor, dead woman. His duty was to see that Lucy didn't suffer the same fate—if they didn't both drown, that is. Jack no longer felt the sharp terror that had been with him in the first days of their captivity. The best he could manage was a dull, oxlike misery.

Olaf moved down the ship, handing out coins to the men.

"Now we're in real trouble," grunted the monk.

"Is he *paying* them?" said Jack, who was so exhausted, he no longer felt pain.

"He's giving them gold so they won't show up empty-handed in the halls of their sea god. Satan will take that gold off them and kick them straight down to Hell." The monk smiled cheerlessly.

Even a little hellfire would be welcome now, Jack thought. The cold made him clumsy, and the bailing bucket kept slipping out of hands. He was so tired, he saw spots before his eyes. He was terrified of fainting. Fainting meant death.

"*Land fyrir stafni!*" someone shouted. A gap in the driving rain showed they were, in fact, quite close to shore. A moment later Jack felt sand under the keel. The oarsmen jumped out and wrestled the boat through the waves to safety.

❖ ❖ ❖

They lay like so many drowned rats on the shore. No one, not even the berserkers, had the strength to move. They had dragged the boat as far from the waves as possible and then collapsed. Jack managed to reach Lucy and held her in his arms. The sea boomed, the wind howled, and rain poured endlessly. In the boat were oilskins to erect as shelters, but no one made a move to unpack them.

Presently, darkness fell. Sunset had not been far off when they came to shore. Jack felt Lucy shudder and tried to dig a hole for her in the sand. At least that would give her some protection from the growing cold. He sat up. A few warriors—Olaf among them—had recovered enough to rise. They bellowed orders, following them with kicks. Slowly, painfully, the captives struggled to their feet. Those who could not were dragged roughly to a field above the tide line.

By now darkness was almost complete. Jack felt a rope being tied around his ankles. He was hobbled to the others, but fortunately, Lucy was not taken from him. He held her close again and, to his relief, felt an oilskin settle over them. The berserkers were not going to lose their cargo to illness.

"There, there," murmured Jack as Lucy continued to shake. His throat felt ragged from shouting over the storm earlier.

"Why won't they take me to my castle?" she said between chattering teeth.

Jack was astounded. Surely she didn't believe that anymore. He paused, uncertain how to answer.

Lucy began to cry. "I keep telling them again and again. They don't listen."

"Dearling, they aren't knights."

"Oh yes they are! Bad ones."

Jack bit his lip and decided to go for the truth. "They're slave traders."

"Don't tell me that!" wailed Lucy. "I don't want to hear it!"

"We have to face it, dearest. We're slaves."

"I don't want to hear it!" She sobbed until her strength was used up. She clung to Jack, shivering and moaning. He couldn't think of a single way to help her. Then, amazingly, Lucy said in a voice that was almost steady, "I know those men aren't knights. I saw that— that poor woman die. I know Thorgil hates me and— and that she'll probably kill me. I'll go to Heaven then, won't I?"

"Of course." Jack's throat felt raw with the urge to cry.

"So that's all right. But until it h-happens, I don't want to think about it. Don't you see? I can't live knowing about it."

And Jack understood. Lucy was like Father. Father was so miserable about his twisted leg, he had to make up stories. Lucy was devastated at being torn from all she had ever known. So was Jack, but he was older. He could stand it. All that stood between Lucy and madness was a thin enchantment of belief. He made a quick decision.

"Most princesses have adventures before they get to their castles," Jack said.

"Sometimes awful ones," said Lucy. She yawned and snuggled close.

"They get carried off by ogres or even fed to dragons. Can you imagine a worse thing than being tied to a tree in front of a deep dark cave?"

"With smoke coming out." Lucy's voice was getting muzzy.

"Black, ugly, foul-smelling smoke."

"But a knight always comes and rescues them."

"Yes, always," said Jack. He blinked back tears. Lucy's hand relaxed its hold on his tunic. Very soon he heard her babyish snores.

He mustn't cry. He mustn't cry. He was all Lucy had, and he mustn't fail her. Jack felt at his neck. The rune of protection spread warmth over his hand and up his arm. Taking care of Lucy wasn't a bad thing, really. It was much better than having no one at all. *How odd,* Jack thought. He had no more control over his life than a dog on a chain, but caring for Lucy made him feel . . . well . . . strong.

I wish the Bard could explain it to me, Jack thought. He sighed and prepared himself for a long night with the rain pounding on the oilskin over their heads.

Dark Reflections Book One: The Water Mirror

by KAI MEYER

Merle and Serafin are catapulted into a wild adventure when they overhear a plot to hand over their beloved Venice to the invading Egyptians. A world of magic and menace unfolds in this daringly original fantasy by a master storyteller. A blockbuster bestseller in Germany, *The Water Mirror* is the first book in a fast-paced trilogy.

KAI MEYER is the author of a number of novels for adults and young adults. *The Water Mirror*, which was nominated for the German Book Prize and was on many bestseller lists in Germany (selling 275,000 copies), has been translated into thirteen languages. Kai Meyer lives in Germany.

Visit www.SimonSaysTEEN.com for more on *Dark Reflections, Book 1: The Water Mirror.*

PUBLISHING EARLY FALL 2005

Margaret K. McElderry Books
New York ✦ London ✦ Toronto ✦ Sydney

↬ 5 ↫

TREACHERY

MERLE AND SERAFIN WALKED FARTHER THROUGH THE maze of narrow alleys and passages, here turning right, there left, crossing bridges over still canals, and going through gateways and along under clotheslines that stretched between the houses like a march of pale ghost sheets. They did not meet one single person along the way, another characteristic of this strangest of old cities: You could walk for miles without seeing a soul, only cats and rats on their hunt for prey in the garbage.

Before them the alley ended at the very edge of a canal. There was no sidewalk along its banks, the walls of the houses reached right down into the water. There wasn't a bridge to be seen.

"A dead end," Merle grumbled. "We have to go back again."

Serafin shook his head. "We're exactly where I wanted to be." He bent over the edge a bit and looked up at the sky. Then he looked across the water. "See that?"

Merle walked up next to him. Her eyes followed his index finger to the gently swelling surface. The brackish smell of the canal rose into her nose, but she hardly noticed it. Strands of algae were drifting about, far more than usual.

An illuminated window was reflected in the water, the only one far and wide. It was in the second floor of a house on the other side of the canal. The opposite bank was about fifty feet away.

"I don't know what you mean," she said.

"See the light in that window?"

"Sure."

Serafin pulled out a silver pocket watch, a valuable piece that probably came from his thieving days. He snapped open the lid. "Ten after twelve. We're on time."

"So?"

He grinned. "I'll explain. You see the reflection on the water, don't you?"

She nodded.

"Good. Now look at the house over it and show me the window that's reflected there. The one that's lit."

Merle looked up at the dark house front. All the windows were dark, not a single one lit. She looked down at the water again. The reflection remained unchanged: In one of the reflected windows a light was burning. When she looked up at the house again, that rectangle in the wall was dark.

"How can that be?" she asked, perplexed. "In the reflection the window is lit, but in reality it's pitch black."

Serafin's grin got even wider. "Well, well."

"Magic?"

"Not entirely. Or maybe yes. Depending on how you look at it."

Her face darkened. "Couldn't you express yourself a little more clearly?"

"It happens in the hour after midnight. Between twelve and one at night the same phenomenon appears at several places in the city. Very few know about them, and even I don't know many of these places, but it's true: During this hour, a few houses cast a reflection on the water that doesn't tally with the reality. There are only tiny differences— lighted windows, sometimes another door, or people walking along in front of the houses while in reality there's nobody there."

"And what does it mean?"

"Nobody knows for sure. But there are rumors." He lowered his voice and acted very mysterious. "Stories about a *second* Venice."

"A second Venice?"

"One that only exists in the reflection in the water. Or at least lies so far away from us that it can't be reached, even with the fastest ship. Not even with the Empire's sunbarks. People say that it's in another world, which is so like ours and yet entirely different. And around midnight the border between the two cities becomes porous, perhaps just because it's so old and has gotten worn over the centuries, like a worn-out carpet."

Merle stared at him, her eyes wide. "You mean, that window with the light . . . you mean, it actually exists—only not *here*?"

"It gets even better. There was an old beggar who sat at this spot for years and watched day and night. He told me that sometimes men and women from this other Venice managed to cross the wall between the worlds. What they don't know, though, is that they're no longer human beings when they arrive here. They're only phantoms then, and they're caught forever in the mirrors of the city. Some of them manage to jump from mirror to mirror, and so every now and then they also stray into your master's workshop and into his magic mirrors."

Merle considered whether Serafin might perhaps be playing a joke on her. "You aren't just trying to put something over on me, are you?"

Serafin flashed a phony smile. "Do I really look as though I could swindle anyone?"

"Of course not, top-notch master thief."

"Believe me, I've actually heard this story. How much of it's the truth, I can't really say." He pointed to the illuminated window in the water. "However, some things support it."

"But that would mean that I was catching human beings in that glass ball the other day!"

"Don't worry about it. I've seen Arcimboldo throw them in the canal. They get out again somehow there."

"And now I understand what he meant when he said that the phantoms could install themselves in the reflections on the water." Merle gasped. "Arcimboldo knows! He knows the truth!"

"What are you going to do now? Ask him about it?"

She shrugged her shoulders. "Why not?" She didn't have a chance to pursue the thought further, for suddenly there was a movement on the water. As they looked down more attentively, a silhouette slid over the surface of the canal toward them.

"Is that—" She broke off as it became clear to her that the reflection was no illusion.

"Back!" Serafin had seen it at the same time.

They whipped into the alleyway and pressed tight against the wall.

From the left, something large glided over the water without touching it. It was a lion with mighty wings of feathers; like the entire body, they were also of stone.

Their tips almost touched the walls of the houses on both sides of the canal. The lion flew almost soundlessly, only its unhurried wingbeats producing subtle whishing like the drawing of breath. Their draft blew icily into Merle's and Serafin's faces. The enormous mass and weight of that body were deceptive; in the air it held itself as featherlight as a bird. Its front and back legs were bent, its mouth nearly closed. Behind its eyes sparkled a disconcerting shrewdness, far sharper than the understanding of ordinary animals.

A soldier sat grimly on the lion's back. His uniform was of black leather and trimmed with steel rivets. A bodyguard of the City Council, assigned to protect one of the big bosses personally. You didn't encounter them very often, and when you did, it usually meant nothing good.

The lion bearing its master floated past the opening of their alleyway without noticing the two of them. Merle and Serafin didn't dare breathe until the flying predator had left them far behind. Carefully they leaned forward and watched the lion gain altitude, leave the narrow canyon of the canal, and make a wide loop over the roofs of the district. Then it was lost to sight.

"He's circling," Serafin stated. "Whoever he's watching can't be far away."

"A councillor?" Merle whispered. "At this hour? In this district? Never in your life. They only leave their palaces when it's absolutely necessary."

"There aren't many lions that can fly. The few that are left never go any farther than necessary from their councillors." Serafin took a deep breath. "One of the councillors must be very close by."

As if to underline his words, the growl of a flying lion came out of the nighttime darkness. A second answered the call. Then a third.

"There are several." Merle shook her head in bafflement. "What are they doing here?"

Serafin's eyes gleamed. "We could find out."

"And the lions?"

"I've often run away from them before."

Merle wasn't sure if he was boasting or telling the truth. Perhaps both. She simply didn't know him well enough. Her instinct told her that she could trust him. *Must* trust him, it looked at the moment—for Serafin had already made his way to the other end of the alleyway.

She hurried after him until she came even with him again. "I hate having to run after other people."

"Sometimes it helps to get decisions made."

She snorted. "I hate it even more when other people want to make my decisions for me."

He stopped and held her back by the arm. "You're right. We both have to want this. It could get quite dangerous."

Merle sighed. "I'm not one of those girls who gives up easily—so don't treat me like one. And I'm not afraid of flying lions." *Of course not,* she said silently to herself, *I've never been chased by one yet either.*

"No reason to be offended now."

"I'm not at all."

"You are so."

"And you keep picking a fight."

He grinned. "Occupational disease."

"Boaster! But you aren't a thief anymore." She left him standing and walked on. "Come on. Or there won't be lions or councillors or adventure tonight."

This time it was he who followed her. She had the feeling that he was testing her. Would she go in the same direction that he'd chosen? Would she interpret the distant wingbeats against the sky properly to lead them to their goal?

She'd show him where to go—literally, in fact.

She hurried around the next corner and kept looking up at the night sky between the edges of the roofs, until she finally slowed and took pains to make no more sound. From here on they ran the danger of being discovered. She just didn't know whether the danger threatened from the sky or from one of the doorways.

"It's that house over there," Serafin whispered.

Her eye followed his index finger to the entrance of a narrow building, just wide enough for a door and two boarded-up windows. It seemed to have once been a servants' annex to one of the neighboring grand houses, in days when the facades of Venice still bore witness to wealth and magnificence. But today many of the palazzi stood just as empty as the houses on the Canal of the Expelled and elsewhere. Not even tramps and beggars squatted there, for in winter the gigantic rooms were impossible to heat. Firewood had been a scarce commodity since the beginning of the siege, and so the stripping of the abandoned buildings of the city had begun long ago, breaking out their wooden floors and beams in order to heat the wood stoves in the cold months.

"How do you know it's this particular house?" Merle asked softly.

Serafin gestured to the roof. Merle had to admit that he had astonishingly good eyes: Something peeked over the edge of the roof, a stone paw, which scratched the tiles. It was impossible to see the lions from the street. Nevertheless, Merle did not doubt that watchful eyes were staring down out of the darkness.

"Let's try around back," Serafin suggested softly.

"But the back side of the house is right on the canal!" Merle's sense of direction in the narrow alleyways was unbeatable. She knew exactly how it looked behind this row of houses. The walls there were smooth, and there was no walk along the edge of the canal.

"We'll manage anyhow," said Serafin. "Trust me."

"As friend or master thief?"

He stopped for a moment, tilted his head, and looked

at her in amazement. Then he stuck out his hand. "Friends?" he asked carefully.

She took his hand firmly in her own. "Friends."

Serafin beamed. "Then I say to you as master thief that somehow we are going to get inside this house. And as friend—" he hesitated, then went on, "as friend I promise you that I will never let you down, no matter what happens tonight."

He didn't wait for her reply but pulled her with him, back into the shadows of the alleyway out of which they had come. Unerringly they made their way through tunnels, across a back courtyard, and through empty houses.

It seemed almost no time until they were edging their way along a narrow ledge that ran along the back of a row of buildings. The pitch-dark water rocked below them. About twenty yards farther, vague in the faint moonlight, the curved outline of a bridge was discernible. And at its highest point stood a lion with an armed rider. If he were to turn around, he would surely be able to spot them in the darkness.

"I hope the lion doesn't sense us," Merle whispered. Like Serafin, she was pressing herself flat against the wall. The ledge was just wide enough for her heels. She had trouble trying to keep her balance and at the same time keep her eye on the sentry on the bridge.

Serafin had less difficulty negotiating the ledge. He was accustomed to getting into strange houses in the most unusual ways, first as a thief, then as Umberto's secret courier. Still, he didn't give Merle the feeling she was holding him back.

"Why doesn't he turn around?" he burst out through clenched teeth. "I don't like that."

Since Merle was a little smaller than he was, she could see a little farther under the bridge. Now she saw that a boat was approaching from the opposite direction. She reported her discovery to Serafin in a whisper. "The guard doesn't seem bothered by it. It looks as though he's been waiting for the boat."

"A secret meeting," Serafin guessed. "I've seen those a few times—a councillor meeting one of his informants. They say the councillors have spies everywhere, in all sorts of people."

Merle had other concerns at the moment. "How much farther is it?"

Serafin bent over a fraction of an inch. "About ten feet, then we're at the first window. If it's open, we can climb into the house." He looked around at Merle. "Can you tell who's in the boat?"

She blinked hard, hoping to be able to see the figure in the bow more clearly. But, like both the oarsmen sitting farther behind him, he was wrapped in a dark hooded cloak. No wonder, considering the time and the cold, and yet Merle shivered at the look of him. Was she mistaken, or did the lion on the bridge paw the ground nervously?

Serafin reached the window. Now they were no more than ten yards away from the bridge. He looked carefully through the glass and nodded to Merle. "The room's empty. They must be waiting somewhere else in the house."

"Can you get the window open?" Merle wasn't really subject to dizziness, but her back had begun to hurt and a tingling was creeping up her outspread legs.

Serafin pressed against the glass, first gently, then a little harder. A slight crack sounded. The right window swung inward on its hinges.

Merle sighed in relief. Thank goodness! She tried to keep her eye on the boat while Serafin climbed into the house. The dinghy had tied up on the other side of the bridge. The lion bore its rider to firm ground to receive the hooded and mantled figure.

Merle saw flying lions in the sky. At least three, perhaps more. If one of them should swoop down again and fly along the canal, he would discover her immediately.

But then Serafin reached his hand to her through the window and pulled her inside the house. She gasped as she felt wooden planks under her feet. She could have kissed the floor with relief. Or Serafin. Better not. She felt her cheeks flush red.

"Are you all right?" he asked.

"I was working hard," she replied quickly and turned away. "What next?"

He took his time answering. At first she thought he was still staring at her; then she realized that he was listening, quite like the way Junipa had listened during their journey along the Canal of the Expelled—highly concentrated, so that not the slightest sound escaped him.

"They're farther front in the house," he said at last. "At least two men, possibly even three."

"With the soldiers that makes it roughly half a dozen."

"Afraid?"

"Not a bit."

He smiled. "*Who's* the boaster here?"

She couldn't help returning his smile. He could see through her, even in the dark. With anyone else that would have made her uncomfortable. "Trust me," he'd said, and in fact, she did trust him. Everything had gone much too fast, but she had no time to worry about it.

Quiet as mice, they slipped out of the room and felt their way down a pitch-black hallway. At its end lay the front door. A shimmer of candlelight was falling through the first corridor on the right. On their left a flight of stairs led up to the second floor.

Serafin brought his lips very close to Merle's ear. "Wait here. I'm going to look around."

She wanted to protest, but he quickly shook his head.

"Please," he added.

With heavy heart she looked after him as he quickly tiptoed to the lighted hallway. At any moment the front door could open and the man in the hooded cape come in, accompanied by the soldiers.

Serafin reached the doorway, looked carefully through it, waited a moment, then turned back to Merle. Dumbly he pointed to the stairs to the upper floor.

She followed his instruction noiselessly. He was the master thief, not she. Perhaps he knew best what to do, even if it was hard for her to admit it. She was unwilling to do what others told her to—whether or not it was in her own best interest.

The stairs were of solid stone. Merle went up and on the second floor made her way to the room that lay over the candlelit room on the ground floor. There she understood what had drawn Serafin upstairs.

A third of the floor had fallen in a long time ago. Wooden beams were scattered and splintered away from the edges, framing a wide opening in the center of the room. From below, candles sent a faint light. Low voices could be heard. Their tone sounded uncertain and apprehensive, even though Merle couldn't make out the exact words.

"Three men," Serafin whispered in her ear. "All three city councillors. Big bosses."

Merle peeked over the edge. She felt the warmth of the light rising to her face. Serafin was right. The three men standing next to one another down there in the light of the candles wore the long robes of Council members, golden and purple and scarlet.

In all of Venice there was no higher authority than the City Council. Since the invasion by the Empire and the loss of all contact with the mainland, they had jurisdiction over the affairs of the besieged city. They had all powers in their hands and they maintained the connection with the Flowing Queen—at least that's what they said. They posed to the public as men of the world and infallible. But among the people, there were guarded whispers of misuse of power, nepotism, and the decadence of the old noble families, to which most of the city councillors belonged. It was no secret that those who had money received preference, and anyone who bore an old family name counted more than ordinary folk.

One of the three men on the ground floor was holding a small wooden box in his hands. It looked like a jewel casket made of ebony.

"What're they doing here?" Merle mouthed silently.

Serafin shrugged his shoulders.

There was a grating sound down below. The front door was opened. There were footsteps, then the voice of a soldier.

"My lords councillor," he announced respectfully, "the Egyptian envoy has arrived."

"For heaven's sake, shut your mouth!" hissed the councillor in the purple robe. "Or do you want the entire district to hear of it?"

The soldier withdrew and left the house, and his companion entered the room. It was the man from the boat, and even now he wore his hood drawn deep over his face. The candlelight wasn't enough to illuminate the shadows under it.

He dispensed with a greeting. "You have carried out what you promised?"

Merle had never heard an Egyptian speak. She was surprised that the man's words showed no accent. But she was too tense to evaluate the significance of the situation right away. Only gradually did its enormous import sink in: a secret meeting between City Council members and an envoy of the Egyptians! A spy, probably, who lived in the city under cover, or otherwise his Venetian dialect wouldn't have been so perfect.

Serafin was chalk white. Drops of sweat beaded his forehead. In shock he peered over the edge into the room below.

The councillor in gold bowed respectfully and the two others did the same after him. "We are glad that you have agreed to this meeting. And certainly, we have carried out what you requested."

The councillor in scarlet nervously clasped his fingers. "The Pharaoh will show himself grateful, won't he?"

With a jerk, the black opening of the hood turned toward him. "God-Emperor Amenophis will learn of your request to join with us. What happens then lies in his divine hands alone."

"Certainly, certainly," the purple councillor hastened to appease him. He cast an angry look toward the man in the scarlet robe. "We do not intend to question any decision of His Divinity."

"Where is it?"

The councillor in gold held the jewel casket out to the envoy. "With most humble greetings to Pharaoh Amenophis. From his loyal servants."

Traitor, thought Merle in utter contempt. *Traitor, traitor, traitor!* It made her really sick to hear the groveling tone of the three city councillors. Or was it just the fear that was turning her stomach?

The envoy took the jewel casket and opened the catch. The councillors exchanged uneasy looks.

Merle bent over farther to better see the contents of the box. Serafin, too, tried to see exactly what was in there.

The casket was lined with velvet, on which lay a little vial of crystal, no longer than a finger. The envoy carefully lifted it out, heedlessly letting the casket fall. It crashed on the floor with a bang. As one, the councillors jumped at the sound.

Between thumb and forefinger the man held the vial up to the opening of his hood, directly against the light of the candles.

"Finally, after all these years!" he murmured absently.

Merle looked at Serafin in amazement. What was so valuable in such a tiny vial?

The councillor in purple raised his hands in a solemn gesture. "It is she, truly. The essence of the Flowing Queen. The charm you placed at our disposal has worked a true wonder."

Merle held her breath and exchanged alarmed looks with Serafin.

"The Pharaoh's alchemists have worked on it for twice ten years," said the envoy coolly. "There was never any doubt that the charm would be effective."

"Of course not, of course not."

The councillor in scarlet, who'd already made himself unpleasantly conspicuous, was rocking excitedly from one foot to the other. "But all your magic wouldn't have helped you if we hadn't declared ourselves ready to perform it in the presence of the Flowing Queen. A servant of the Pharaoh would never have gotten so near her."

The envoy's tone turned wary. "So, are you then *not* a servant of the Pharaoh, Councillor de Angeliis?"

The other's face went white. "Certainly I am, certainly, certainly."

"You are nothing but a whining coward. And of those the worst kind: a traitor!"

The councillor wrinkled his nose defiantly. He shook off the hand that the councillor in purple tried to place soothingly on his arm. "Without us you'd never—"

"Councillor de Angeliis!" scolded the envoy, and now he sounded like an angry old woman. "You will receive recompense for your service of friendship, if that is your concern. At the latest when the Pharaoh makes his entrance into the lagoon with his armies and confirms you as his representative in office. But now, in Amenophis's name, will you be quiet!"

"With your permission," said the councillor in purple, paying no attention to the wretched-looking de Angeliis, "you should know that time is pressing. Recently a messenger from Hell has arrived to offer us a pact against the Empire. I don't know how long we can continue to resist that. Others on the City Council are more receptive to this messenger than we are. It won't be possible to hold them in check indefinitely. Especially as the messenger has said that next time he'll appear in public so that *all* the people will learn of his demands."

The envoy expelled his breath in a wheeze. "That must not happen. The attack on the lagoon is imminent. A pact with Hell can bring it all to nothing." He was silent a moment as he considered the situation. "If the messenger actually appears, make sure that he can't get to the people. Kill him."

"And the vengeance of Hell—" de Angeliis began in a subdued voice, but the third councillor motioned him to silence with a wave.

"Certainly, sir," said the councillor in gold, with a bow in the direction of the envoy. "As you command. The Empire will protect us from all consequences when it once has the city under its control."

The Egyptian nodded graciously. "So shall it be."

Merle's lungs desperately demanded air—she couldn't hold her breath one second longer. The sound was soft, barely audible, but still loud enough to alert the councillor in scarlet. He looked up at the hole in the ceiling. Merle and Serafin pulled their heads back just in time. So they only heard the envoy's further words but couldn't see what was going on.

"The desert crystal of the vial is strong enough to hold the Flowing Queen. Her regency over the lagoon is ended. An army of many thousands of soldiers stands ready on land and on the water. As soon as the Pharaoh holds this vial in his hands, the galleys and sunbarks will strike."

Merle felt a movement at her right side. She looked around, but Serafin was too far away. However, something was moving at her hip! A rat? The truth first hit her when it was already too late.

The water mirror slid out of her dress pocket like something alive, with jerky, clumsy movements like a blinded animal. Then everything went at breakneck speed. Merle tried to grab the mirror, but it shot underneath her hand, skidded to the edge of the hole in the floor, slipped out over it—and fell.

In a long moment, as if frozen in time, Merle saw that the surface of the mirror had become milky, fogged by the presence of the phantom.

The mirror plunged past Merle's outstretched hand

into the depths. It fell exactly on the envoy, missed his hood, struck his hand, and knocked the crystal vial out of his fingers. The man howled, with pain, with rage, with surprise, as the mirror and the vial landed on the floor almost at the same time.

"No!" Serafin's cry made the three councillors leap away from each other like drops of hot fat. With a daring bound he swung himself over the edge and sprang into the middle of them. Merle had no time to consider this sudden chain of catastrophes. She followed Serafin over the edge, her dress fluttering around her, and with a loud bellow that was intended to sound grim but was probably anything but.

The envoy avoided her. Otherwise her feet would have hit his head. Hastily he bent and tried to pick up the vial. But his fingers reached past the vial and brushed across the water mirror. For a fraction of a second his fingertips furrowed the surface, vanished under it—and were gone when the envoy pulled back his hand with a scream of pain. Instead of fingertips there were black slivers of bone, which stuck out of the remainders of his fingers, smoking and burned, as if he'd stuck his hand in a beaker of acid.

A mad shrieking came from under the hood. The sound was inhuman because no face appeared to give it; the screaming poured from an invisible mouth.

Serafin did a cartwheel on both hands, almost too fast for the eye to see. When he came to a stop by the window, he held the vial in his right hand and Merle's mirror in his left.

Meanwhile the councillor in purple, the traitors' spokesman, had grabbed Merle by the upper arm and tried to pull her around. With balled fist he raised his arm to strike her, while the two other councillors ran around like frightened hens, bellowing loudly for their bodyguards. Merle dodged him and was able to shake his hand off her arm, but as she did so her back thumped against black stuff. The robe of the envoy. There was a stench of burned flesh around him.

A sharp draft whistled through the cracks of the boarded-up windows: Flying lions had landed outside in front of the house. Steel scraped over steel as sabers were withdrawn from their sheaths.

Someone placed an arm around Merle from behind, but she ducked away under it as she had already in so many scraps in the orphanage. She'd had practice in fighting, and she knew what she had to hit so that it hurt. When Councillor de Angeliis put himself in her way, she placed a well-aimed kick. The fat man in the scarlet robe bellowed as if he'd been spitted, holding his lower abdomen with both hands.

"Out!" cried Serafin, holding the two other councillors in check by threatening to smash the vial on the floor—whatever that might bring about.

Merle raced over to him and ran at his side to the exit.

They turned into the corridor at the very moment the front door burst open and two bodyguards in black leather thundered in.

"By the Ancient Traitor!" Serafin cursed.

Nonplussed, the soldiers stopped in their tracks. They had expected with a trick by the Egyptian, with men armed to the teeth, worthy opponents for two battle-hardened heroes of the Guard. Instead they saw a girl in a ragged dress and a boy who held in his hands two gleaming objects that looked not at all like knives.

Merle and Serafin used the moment of surprise. Before the guards could react, the two were on their way to the back room.

There, in front of the open window, the envoy was waiting for them. He had known that there was only one way of escape. At the back, out to the water.

"The mirror!" Merle called to Serafin.

He threw it over to her, and she caught it with both hands, grabbed it by the handle, and hit at the envoy with it. He avoided it skillfully, but that also left the way to the window free. His singed fingertips still smoked.

"The vial!" he demanded in a hissing voice. "You are setting yourselves against the Pharaoh!"

Serafin let out a daredevil laugh that surprised even Merle. Then he somersaulted past the envoy, between his outstretched hands. He landed safely on the windowsill and sat there like a bird, with both feet on the frame, knees drawn up, and a wide grin on his lips.

"All honor to the Flowing Queen!" he cried out, while Merle used the moment to spring to his side. "Follow me!"

With that he let himself fall backward out the window into the waters of the still canal.

It wasn't really his hand that drew Merle after him: It was his enthusiasm, his sheer will not to give up. For the first time in her life she felt admiration for another person.

The envoy screeched and grabbed the edge of Merle's dress, but it was with the fingers of his eroded hand, and he let go again with a yelp of pain.

The water was icy. In a single heartbeat it seemed to pierce her clothes, her flesh, her entire body. Merle could no longer breathe, nor move, nor even think. She didn't know how long this condition lasted—it seemed to her like minutes—but when she surfaced, Serafin was beside her, and life came back to her limbs. She couldn't have been under for more than a few seconds.

"Here, take this!" Underwater he pressed the vial into her left hand. In the right she was still holding the mirror, which lay between her fingers as if it grew there.

"What shall I do with it?"

"If worse comes to worst, I'll steer them away," said Serafin and spat water. The waves slapped at his lips.

Worse comes to worst, Merle thought. Even worse?

May Bird and the
Ever After

by *Jodi Lynn Anderson*

When May falls into a lake, she finds herself in the ghostly realm of The Ever After—but will she make it out alive? *The Wizard of Oz* meets *Beetlejuice* and *Alice in Wonderland* in this novel—the first of three featuring the adventures of May Bird.

JODI LYNN ANDERSON grew up in New Jersey, where she spent a lot of time walking in the woods, pretending she was a queen. Today she lives in Roswell, Georgia, and spends a lot of time wishing she had a cat.

Visit www.SimonSaysKids.com for more on *May Bird and the Ever After*.

PUBLISHING EARLY FALL 2005

Atheneum Books for Young Readers
New York ✦ London ✦ Toronto ✦ Sydney

A Sack of Beans

AINT AGATHA'S BOARDING SCHOOL FOR GIRLS WITH HIGH
SOCKS. May Ellen Bird, age ten, occasionally glanced at
the brochure her mom had taped to her door that afternoon, and scowled. A few minutes ago May had taken her black
marker and written the word "socks" over what had originally
been the last word of the headline. Judging by the photos of girls
in stiff plaid uniforms plastering the brochure, girls with "high
prospects" was not nearly as accurate.

The woods watched silently through the farthest east window
of White Moss Manor as May tried to concentrate on her work.
And sometimes, looking up from the curious project strewn
across her desk, chewing on a pencil, May watched them back.

Skinny and straight, with short black bobbed hair and big
brown eyes, May ran her fingers over the objects before her—a
clump of black fur, a light bulb, a jar, a book titled *Secrets of the
Egyptian Mummies,* and some wire. Occasionally May swiveled to
gaze at Somber Kitty, who laid across her bed like a discarded
piece of laundry. His belly faced the ceiling and he eyed her
lazily.

Neither May nor Somber Kitty knew it, but passing squirrels and chipmunks thought the cat was decidedly ugly. He had huge pointy ears and a skinny tail, and he was mostly bald, with just a little bit of fuzz covering his soft skin. His mouth was turned down in a thoughtful frown—an expression he had been wearing ever since May had gotten him three years before, on her seventh birthday.

May had disliked him immediately.

"He's bald," she'd said.

"He's a hairless rex," her mom had replied. "He's interesting."

"He looks depressed."

"He's *somber.*"

May's mom had then explained that somber meant sad, which also meant melancholy. So that was the one thing they both agreed on. The cat was most definitely sad. It was almost as if, from the moment he had set his tilty green eyes on May, he had sensed her disappointment in him, and sympathized.

May had wanted him, of course. Her first cat, Legume, had died when May was six, and she had resigned herself to a life of grief. She knew there could never be another Legume, which, by the way, is another word for *peanut.* She'd insisted on wearing black ever since.

But her mom had insisted on another pet. "You spend too much time alone," she had said with big, brown, worried eyes even bigger and browner than May's. Mrs. Bird had long ago given up trying to get May to bring home friends from school.

"Why don't you invite Maribeth over?"

"She has the chicken pox."

"Claire?"

"She's only allowed out on President's Day."

"Mariruth?"

"Leprosy. It's so sad."

Finally one afternoon May had stood in her mom's doorway, crossed her arms, and announced that she would accept a cat, as long as it was a black tiger.

Noticing her watching him now, he opened his mouth and asked, "Mew? Meow? Meay?"

"That's my name, don't wear it out," May replied.

Knock knock knock.

May's mom poked her head into the room.

"So what do you think?" she asked hopefully, smiling. "It looks like a great school, doesn't it?"

May crossed her arms over her waist and looked toward her bed. "Maybe if you're a nun," she offered thoughtfully.

The smile on Mrs. Bird's face dropped, and May felt her heart drop too.

"Maybe it's okay," May added. She looked at Somber Kitty who looked at her. Their traded glance said Somber Kitty understood, even if Mrs. Bird didn't: May could never be happy at a school like Saint Agatha's, wearing high socks and stuck in New York City without the woods.

She ducked into the room, stooped down, and made her way to May's desk. From the ceiling hung a number of objects: a dragonfly wind chime, a clothes hanger strung with old sumac leaves, old dry strands of ivy. At the window sat a pair of binoculars to watch for insects and critters, and a telescope aimed at the sky for looking at the stars.

The walls were so covered in pictures that you couldn't see the old calico wallpaper. They were drawings of Legume, of Mrs. Bird, of the woods, and of imaginary places and friends and creatures: some with wings and purple hair, black capes and horns, and one particularly spooky one with a lopsided head. There were none of Somber Kitty, who often followed Mrs. Bird's eyes to the wall with hurt curiosity, searching for a likeness of himself.

Studying the spookier, darker pictures, Mrs. Bird's eyes sometimes got big and worried again. "You don't want people to think you're eccentric," she'd say, looking more somber than a certain cat.

"You ready for the picnic?" Mrs. Bird asked, walking up behind May and hugging her tight.

May nodded, tugging at the tassels of the sari she'd wrapped around her body like a dress. Because Briery Swamp was too small and empty to have a Day, May and Mrs. Bird always attended the annual Hog Wallow Day Extravaganza and Picnic. It was two towns away, but it involved a parade and games and seeing all the kids from school. "Yep," she replied, trying to sound bright.

Mrs. Bird kissed the top of May's head, her jasmine perfume sinking into May's sari.

"Your classmates will be happy to see you."

May blushed. She doubted it.

May didn't mention that since school let you, she had made improvements—*in secret*—getting ready for this exact day. She had gained two pounds, eating sesame-and-peanut-butter balls two at a time, so she wasn't *quite* so skinny. Her knees didn't look as knobby as they had. And she had worked on her smile in the mirror. Usually May's smile looked like a grimace. But she'd gotten it to look halfway normal, she thought. Girls with nice smiles made friends. Mrs. Bird liked to remind May of this when she came to volunteer on hot-dog days and saw how May sat at the end of the fifth-grade table, curled over her carrots.

"I don't know how to make friends," May would say, embarrassed.

"Well, actually, you don't really *make* friends," Mrs. Bird always replied. "You just have to let them happen."

May didn't think that was very helpful.

"What are you making now?" Mrs. Bird asked.

May surveyed the pieces in front of her. "A materializer. It makes things you imagine real. Like if you imagine a pair of emerald earrings, it makes the earrings appear."

Mrs. Bird crouched, moved back toward the door, then turned a thoughtful gaze on May "Maybe you should be a lawyer someday-then you can make enough money to get me those earrings *for real*" May glanced at the materializer. It was *supposed* to be for real.

"You'd better get a quick bath. I'll run the water."

May lounged on her bed, picturing what it would be like if she went to the picnic today, and her classmates couldn't recognize her with the extra two pounds, and her classmates couldn't recognize her with the extra two pounds and the big, real-looking smile pasted on her face.

Who's that girl? One of the boys, Finny Elway, would say. *She reminds me of May.*

"They'd see the best me," May said aloud to Somber Kitty.

"Meow," the cat replied with interest.

A few minutes later Mrs. Bird's footsteps sounded on the stairs again, then came the squeak of the spigot being turned off, and the footsteps retreating. May stripped off her sari, got naked, and walked out into the hall for her bath. Just outside the bathroom door, she paused. Inside she could hear the splish splash of the water being swirled around the tub.

May grasped the ceramic door handle and twisted it, opening on an empty room, in the middle a white tub with claw feet, with water gently waving back and forth. Leaning over, she inspected it, then climbed in. May was used to strange things like this. Her mom had always said all sorts of quirks came with a house as old as theirs. May used to insist it was ghosts. But Mrs. Bird had long ago given her one too many stern looks on the topic. So May simply sank beneath the water and let bubbles drift out of her of nose.

When she stepped out of the bathroom in a towel a half an hour later, the steam poured out behind her, engulfing the tiny figure of Somber Kitty, who waited in the doorway, licking his paws one by one. With the cat at her heels, May walked into her room and pulled on the turquoise tank top and shorts her mom had laid out instead of the usual black.

Last summer May had built a tiny shelf that snaked its way around the whole room, way up high. Along the sill was the collection of quartz rocks she'd carefully picked from the woods. Her mom swore they were worthless, but they seemed as dazzling and precious as diamonds to May. There was also a complete zoo of lopsided animals she'd made out of paper clips, a perfect heart-shaped pinecone she and Somber Kitty had found together in town, and an onyx brooch left behind by the lady who'd once lived here before them—a lady by the name of Bertha.

The quartz rocks stared at her as if they, too, wanted to go wherever she was headed. Once she was dressed she pulled the smallest one off the shelf and let it hitch a ride in her pocket, for luck.

The picnic was a disaster.

Sweaty and red-faced, May Bird spent much of the afternoon pedaling around the lawn of Hog Wallow Town Hall on a bike with tassels flapping from the handlebars and a stowaway rex cat who'd insisted on coming tucked into her backpack. She'd spotted a gaggle of classmates across the grass, talking and laughing.

It took awhile May to work up the courage to approach her classmates, who stood in a gaggle, talking and laughing. She kept herself busy, scaring crickets out of the grass, then sat against a tree near the picnic table where mothers had gathered, working on her smile.

She overheard the parents talking. "Thank you, we love the house. We're always getting offers," Mrs. Bird was saying, adjusting her hat in a familiar way. She had always said the sun on her face gave her wrinkles. "But I think May needs to be somewhere more . . . average." May's mom looked down at her hands while she said this. Unseen, May blushed. She knew that the reason her mom wanted to move was because she thought *May* needed to be more average. At that moment, Mrs. Bird's eyes drifted toward May's direction, and widened, embarrassed.

May pretended she hadn't noticed, plucked grass between her fingers, and then stood up. Without looking up she made her way toward the other kids.

Pollen blew across the grass, and Somber Kitty nipped at her heels She lifted him up, frowning at him. "I'm going to hang out with the humans," she said. "Go play." He kissed her, his tiny pink tongue darting out to tickle her chin, before she placed him on the grass and gave him a pat on the butt to shoo him away. She nervously straightened out her clothes and made her way against the breeze to where the children had huddled into a tight group. There she tacked herself to the circle awkwardly, like a losing try at pin the tail on the donkey.

Claire Arneson stood at the center of the group of kids. Instead of being pulled into the usual pigtails, her hair was down and combed across her back, shimmery as mountain water. Two bright, pink-ribboned barrettes held back her bangs. May had always wondered why she couldn't be more like Claire, when Claire made being herself seem so easy. She always had something funny to say. She never looked big-eyed and serious. And she had a million friends, none of whom were bald cats.

"I'm only allowed to have eight people," Claire was saying, "Maribeth's coming, and Colleen. . . . Finny, can you come?"

May smiled big as Claire singled out the kids that would attend her annual Kites and Katydids birthday party. Maybe they hadn't even recognized her yet. Maybe Claire would invite her to the party, thinking she was inviting a mysterious stranger.

"Hey, May . . ."

May brightened and nodded as Claire turned to her, her heart doing a jig in her chest. "Isn't that your dancing cat?" Claire pointed one perfect finger across the lawn and all eyes followed.

Oh. Disappointment. "Yes." May tried her nongrimace smile again. It felt like the old one, grimacelike.

The whole class remembered Somber Kitty because May had

brought him in for her "How To" report in February. Everyone else had done their reports on things like "How to Make a Bologna Sandwich" and "How to Sew a Pillow." May had done hers on "How to Teach Your Cat to Dance." It was one of the few times May's classmates had actually noticed she was alive in a good way. (They'd noticed her in a bad way many times.) It had also sort of been cheating, because Somber Kitty, despite his general sadness, loved to dance and had known how since he was a kitten.

"That was so cool!" Finny Elway said.

May cleared her throat, her disappointment fading. They thought she had a cool cat.

"Yeah," Elmore Smith said. "But the best was when May tried to fly off the roof of her mom's car with that bunch of balloons, remember?" Everyone burst into giggles. May's heart sank. She tried to smile, as if she was in on the joke. She rubbed at the scar on her knee from that incident, which had happened at last year's picnic. Ever since then she'd been afraid of heights.

"Hey, remember May Bird, Warrior Princess?" Maribeth asked. Now the laughter exploded, and May began to really and truly blush, remembering the day the photo had fallen out of her social studies textbook onto the floor. It had been a shot of her and Somber Kitty pretending to be Amazon warriors hiding in the trees. In it, May had on her black sparkly bathing suit that made her feel like she was wearing the night sky, and a belt wrapped around her shoulder with long sticks tucked beneath the strap for arrows. Mrs. Bird had said May shouldn't dress like a half-naked wild thing, but she had stuck the photo into one of May's notebooks to surprise her and make her smile. It *had* surprised her by falling out. It *hadn't* made her smile. It had made her want to sink into the gold and green tiles of the school floor.

"Remember when May forgot to lock the bathroom door on the bus trip, and it swung open?"

May shifted from foot to foot, looking at the ground to hide her flaming face. She gazed toward the adults' table helplessly, wanting to make sure her mom couldn't see. Luckily Mrs. Bird was still busy talking with the other grown-ups.

It was the three-legged race that saved her. The mayor of Hog Wallow announced that everyone was to line up across the lawn by the pink flag.

No sooner had he said it than, shouting and laughing, the children went tearing across the grass. Dazed, May dragged after them, her long skinny legs straggling. Races were her favorite. She was deadly fast.

But you needed a partner for a three-legged race. And everyone paired up without her.

"Mew? Meow? Meay?" Somber Kitty asked, appearing out of nowhere and rubbing against her shins.

"Cats can't race," May said with a sigh. They watched the racers line up, and then the starting bell went off, and Claire and Maribeth pulled out in front. They were way slower than May would have been. But May would have traded her speed for a partner to race with.

She turned around and walked back to her bike, far away from the crowd, and plopped down next to it in the grass.

"I think if I could go somewhere else, I could be someone else," she whispered to her cat. She picked a puffy white dandelion out of the grass between her sandals and blew at the seeds.

Somber Kitty, who always seemed to know May had no one else to tell her feelings to, mewed in agreement, though he had no idea what she was saying.

"But that doesn't mean I want to move to New York," she quickly added.

Then she slumped. She felt as heavy as a sack of beans. But then, a sack of beans never got embarrassed or did stupid balloon tricks in front of other sacks of beans, or forget to lock the bathroom door. Come to think of it, life was probably easy for all the beans of the world. Being a sack of them wouldn't be so bad.

May picked another dandelion and blew on it. "Maybe I'd rather be a sack of beans," she told the fuzzy white floaters. Somber Kitty meowed disapprovingly.

"Don't worry, Kitty. I'm not going anywhere."

Somber Kitty rolled himself into a ball and continued to stare at her. He didn't look so sure.

"Unless you know something I don't."

At the edge of the grass, the trees watched her.

They knew better.

A Letter from Before

YOU CAN DROP ME OFF HERE."

Mrs. Bird looked at May, then at the dirt road ahead of them, then back at May, who sat with her back straight the way her mom always asked her to. Mrs. Bird ran her free hand through her wavy brown hair as she brought the car to a stop.

"You sure you don't want to just come home, pumpkin?"

May nodded.

"I wish you wouldn't spend so much time in the woods. I worry about snakes."

May opened the door, but felt her mom's hand on her back. She turned. "I love you, pumpkin," Mrs. Bird said.

"You too."

"Wait, May?"

May was halfway out of the car, when she ducked back down to meet her mom's eyes. "You know I wouldn't trade you for anybody in the world, right?"

May smiled. Mrs. Bird seemed to breath a sigh of relief before

May closed the door and went around to the back of the car to get her bike and her backpack, Somber Kitty jumped out of the back too, just before May closed the door and the car pulled away.

"Thank God," May said. She looked around the dilapidated and deserted square of Briery Swamp. Except for being dry and dead, it looked like any other town in the state of West Virginia.

May Bird had always thought that if states were like people, West Virginia would be the shy relative of, say, Texas. Texas was big and bad and sprawled out flat, saying "Look at me, I'm Texas!" West Virginia was mysterious and it liked to keep to itself. It hid in the folds of mountains, resting in the cool shade. It was sweet, beautiful and bashful. Its woods held its secrets, or at least it seemed that way to May.

Briery Swamp wasn't much of a town anymore. The houses that had once stood in a sociable gaggle at the town square had crumbled into crooked piles of bricks, overgrown with weeds. A possum, four snakes, and a hundred thousand three hundred and six earthworms had moved into what used to be the mayor's graceful mansion. The postmaster's old cottage was the centipedes' favorite place for hatching long crawly babies.

The only building in town that still looked like a building at all was the post office itself. It stood up from the weeds like a snaggle tooth, three of its walls mostly collapsed and pouring onto the grass like a waterfall.

May laid her bike on its side and stared around. There wasn't much to do except meander around the square with Somber Kitty and tell him made-up stories about the people who'd lived here, and why they'd moved away. Since there had been a drought in

Briery Swamp for as long as she could remember, her favorite theory was that the rain had retired to Florida, and all the people of Briery Swamp had followed it there.

"Meow," Somber Kitty said, which May interpreted to mean "At least we have each other." The pair spent an hour or more kicking rocks up and down the road, until Somber Kitty ran off into the woods chasing a moth. Then, for the millionth time, May ducked in through the hole in the old post office wall and began digging through the rocks for treasures. Once she'd found a stuffed skunk mounted on a plaque. She'd also found three old rubber stamps saying "First Class," "Second Class," and "Third Class."

Now she thrust her hands into a pile of rubble against the back wall, sifting out the larger rocks from the smaller ones, hoping to find maybe another stamp, or an old letter. She was just digging in with one last thrust when her fingers lit on something that felt distinctly different from rubble. It felt like paper. May pinched with her thumb and forefinger and gently extracted it, watching a corner of molded white emerge from the pile. It slid out with a little scratch.

It *was* a letter. A huge find. May couldn't believe her luck.

"Meay?"

"Oh, you scared me," May said, her heart racing as she met Somber Kitty's tilty green eyes. "Look at this."

May held the letter up for the cat to see. "Somebody didn't get their mail." She ran her tongue against the inside of her bottom lip, thinking. "Maybe it's some private stuff," she whispered breathlessly to the cat, who had already gotten bored on the letter and started licking his black paws.

The envelope was clearly very old—yellowed with age. One corner was folded back so that the stamp and postmark were visible. Though it was faded, May could just make out the date: June 11, 1951.

"I hope they weren't holding their breath," May said with a small, curious smile. A slant of light found its way through the hole in the wall and striped her face, making her look like two halves of herself. Where the flap of the envelope ended in a point there was a faded stamp of a tree surrounded by snowflakes and, when May looked closer, the face of an old woman, peering through the leaves. May stared at the stamp for a long time, a knot of unease gathering beneath her ribs. It was one of the prettiest pictures she'd ever seen, but her gut didn't like it. She had to think for a minute to figure out why, but then she had it. The thing about it was that you couldn't tell if the person who'd drawn it had meant for the lady to be a nice, old woman, inviting you into the tree, or someone not so nice, waiting to pounce on you like . . . a tiger. May knew one thing: She was grateful she'd never have to find out.

Letting out her breath, she turned the letter over, rubbed at the dust and mold covering the address, and froze. She blinked twice. She read the words in front of her three times, her eyes as wide as cereal bowls.

The envelope, in blue, loopy letters, read:

> Miss May Ellen Bird
> White Moss Manor
> Briery Swamp, WV

"Meay?" May jolted, her eyes shooting to Somber Kitty, who'd snuck up beside her.

"Shh, Kitty."

She patted the cat's head absently, then returned her gaze to the letter. She looked at the seal on the back, then turned it over again to look at the address. *Her* address. She felt like a firefly was lighting her up from the inside out. She stood up and looked around, then sat down again.

It had to be a different May Bird.

But then, there was her address.

May chewed on a finger, thinking hard. The date had to be wrong. Nineteen fifty-one. May didn't even think her *mom* had been born then.

But if the date was wrong, and the letter was sent recently, then how did it end up buried under all the old bricks of the post office?

May turned the letter over again and again and again, trying to make sure she was really seeing it.

"Well, Kitty," she whispered, "what do you think we should do?"

May bit her lip, then raised a pinky to her mouth and began nibbling just the tip. She lowered her fingers to the slit in the back of the envelope to open it, then changed her mind and stopped, then started again. Once she started, she ripped it open with lightning speed.

There was nothing strange about the letter itself, except what was written on it. It was a single sheet of yellowed paper, just like an old letter should be, mottled with blue swirls and waves where the paper had gotten wet, making the ink bleed and blur. May pulled it out gingerly, worried it might disintegrate. She unfolded it.

Dear Miss Bird,

The Lady of North Farm had asked us to send you this map to Briery Swamp Lake, just in case. She thought you might be having trouble finding it on your own, and she is expecting you to be prompt. We are very sorry for the danger you will endure, but we eagerly await your arrival should you survive it, as we are in great need of your help. The Lady joins me in sending you good luck and best wishes.

Sincerely,

Ms. H. Kari Kagaki
T.E.A. Travel

May let out a sigh of relief. That settled it. She didn't know Kari Kagaki or any North Farm. They had the wrong person. She sank back, feeling like a casserole dish full of Jell-O. She looked at the envelope and the picture again. It brought back that uneasy knot.

May's fingers stretched toward the map, and she looked at it sideways, trying to pretend that she wasn't looking at all. She immediately recognized a few things. There was the town square. There-the knot got worse-was White Moss Manor, and there were the woods. The map even showed a dark smudge, where the giant gathering of briers-the Endless Briers, May called them, because she'd never managed to cross them-wound their way thickly along the east side of May's woods.

And beyond them, there was a lake.

Even more than the letter itself, this couldn't be believed. There were no lakes in Briery swamp. Not even a puddle. The squirrels and chipmunks, May had always supposed, went to the next town over to get their water. If the lake had been there in 1951, it wasn't there now.

May crumbled up the letter and dropped it on the ground. But as soon as she stood up, she swept down and picked it up. Turning red, she flattened the letter out, folded it, and tucked it into her knapsack. She caught Somber Kitty looking at her thoughtfully.

"I don't want to litter," she said, knowing there wasn't a thing in the world that would get her to go looking for that lake. But Somber Kitty didn't appear to be convinced. May sighed. "Really."

The truth was, nobody had ever said they needed her.

"Mew," was all she got in reply from someone who needed her very much. If a cat-to-English dictionary had been handy, and May had looked up "mew," it would have translated into something like "Curiosity killed the cat."

"We shouldn't tell anybody. It'll be our secret."

May climbed onto her bike, held her knapsack down for the cat to crawl into, and together they headed home.

#1 The Field Guide

by TONY DITERLIZZI AND HOLLY BLACK

When the Grace children take up residence in their great aunt's Victorian house and discover a strange old book, they uncover a world filled with elves, goblins, dwarves, trolls, and other fantastical creatures. *The Field Guide* is the first book in this number-one *New York Times* and *USA Today* bestselling series.

TONY DiTERLiZZi is also the illustrator of the Caldecott Honor–winning *The Spider and the Fly* by Mary Howitt. He lives in Amherst, Massachusetts, with his wife, Angela, and their pug, Goblin.

HOLLY BLACK is also the author of *Valiant: A Modern Tale of Faerie* (available June 2005), a follow-up to her first book, *Tithe: A Modern Faerie Tale*, which published in fall 2002 to stellar reviews. She lives with her husband, Theo, in Amherst, Massachusetts.

Please visit www.SimonSaysKids.com/spiderwick or www.spiderwick.com for Spiderwick games, an interview with Tony and Holly, downloadable trading cards, and more creature features!

Simon & Schuster Books for Young Readers
New York ✦ London ✦ Toronto ✦ Sydney

The creak startled him into jerking upright.

Chapter Two

IN WHICH Two Walls Are Explored by Vastly Different Methods

The leaks in the roof had made all but three of the upstairs bedroom floors dangerously rotted. Their mother got one, Mallory got another, and Jared and Simon were left to share the third.

By the time they were done unpacking, the dressers and nightstands of Simon's side of the room were covered in glass tanks. A few were filled with fish. The rest were crammed with mice, lizards, and other animals that Simon had confined to mud-furnished cages. Their mother

MALLORY GRACE

had told Simon he could bring everything but the mice. She thought they were disgusting because Simon had rescued them from a trap in Mrs. Levette's downstairs apartment. She pretended not to notice he'd brought them anyway.

Jared tossed and turned on the lumpy mattress, pressing the pillow down over his head like he was smothering himself, but he couldn't sleep. He didn't mind sharing a room with Simon, but sharing a room with cages of animals that rustled, squeaked, and scratched was eerier than sleeping alone would have been. It made him think of the thing in the walls. He'd shared a room with Simon and the critters in the city, but the animal noises had dimmed against the background of cars and sirens and people. Here, everything was unfamiliar.

The creak of hinges startled him into jerking upright. There was a figure in the doorway, with a shapeless white gown and long, dark hair. Jared slid off the bed so fast he didn't even remember doing it.

"It's just me," the figure whispered. It was Mallory in a nightgown. "I think I heard your squirrel."

Jared stood up from a crouch, trying to decide if moving so fast meant he was a chicken or if he just had good reflexes. Simon was snoring gently in the other bed.

Mallory put her hands on her hips. "Come on. It's not going to wait around for us to catch it."

Jared shook his twin's shoulder. "Simon. Wake up. New pet. New peeeeeeeeeet."

Simon twitched and groaned, trying to pull the covers over his head.

Mallory laughed.

"Simon." Jared leaned in close, making his voice deliberately urgent. "Squirrel! Squirrel!"

Simon opened his eyes and glared at them. "I was sleeping."

"Mom went out to the store for milk and cereal," Mallory said, pulling the covers off him. "She said I was supposed to keep an eye on you. We don't have much time before she gets back."

The three siblings crept along the dark hallways of their new house. Mallory was in the lead, walking a few paces and then stopping to listen. Every now and then there would be a scratch or a sound like small footsteps inside the walls.

The scuttling grew louder as they neared the kitchen. In the kitchen sink, Jared could see a pan crusted with the remains of the macaroni and cheese they'd had for dinner.

"I think it's there. Listen," Mallory whispered.

The sound stopped completely.

Mallory picked up a broom and held the wooden end like a baseball bat. "I'm going to knock open the wall," she said.

"Mom is going to see the hole when she gets back," Jared said.

"In this house? She'll never notice."

"What if you hit the squirrel?" Simon asked. "You could hurt—"

"Shhhh," Mallory said. She padded across the floor in her bare feet and swung the broom handle at the wall. The blow broke through the plaster, scattering dust like flour. It settled in Mallory's hair, making her look even more ghostly. She reached into the hole and broke off a chunk of the wall.

Jared stepped closer. He could feel the hair on his arms stand up.

Torn strips of cloth had been wadded up between the boards. As she snapped off more pieces, other things were revealed. The remains of curtains. Bits of tattered silk and lace. Straight pins poked into the wooden beams on either side, making a strange upward-snaking line. A doll's head lolled in one corner. Dead cockroaches were strung up like garlands. Tiny lead soldiers with melted hands and feet were scattered across the planks like a fallen army.

"I'm going to knock open the wall."

Jagged pieces of mirror glittered from where they had been glued with ancient gum.

Mallory reached into the nest and took out a fencing medal. It was silver with a thick blue ribbon. "This is mine."

"The squirrel must have stolen it," said Simon.

"No—this is too weird," Jared said.

"Dianna Beckley had ferrets, and they used to steal her Barbie dolls," Simon replied. "And lots of animals like shiny things."

"But look." Jared pointed to the cockroaches. "What ferret makes his own gross knickknacks?"

"Let's pull this stuff out of here," Mallory

said. "Maybe if it doesn't have a nest, it will be easier to keep out of the house."

Jared hesitated. He didn't want to put his hands inside the wall and feel around. What if it was still in there and bit him? Maybe he didn't know much, but he really didn't think squirrels were normally this creepy. "I don't think we should do that," he said.

Mallory wasn't listening. She was busy dragging over a trash can. Simon started pulling out wads of the musty cloth.

"There's no droppings, either. That's strange." Simon dumped what he was holding and pulled out another handful. At the army men, he stopped. "These are cool, aren't they, Jared?"

Jared had to nod. "They'd be better with hands, though."

Simon put several in the pocket of his pajamas.

"Simon?" Jared asked. "Have you ever heard of an animal like this? I mean, some of this stuff is really odd, you know? Like this squirrel must be as demented as Aunt Lucy."

"Yeah, it's real nutty," Simon said, and giggled.

Mallory groaned, then suddenly went quiet. "I hear it again."

"What?" Jared asked.

"The noise. Shhhh. It's over there." Mallory picked up the broom again.

"Quiet," Simon whispered.

"We're being quiet," Mallory hissed back.

"Shush," Jared said.

The three of them crept over to where the sound came from, just as the noise itself changed. Instead of hearing the clatter of little claws scrabbling on wood, they could clearly hear the scrape of nails on metal.

"Look." Simon bent down to touch a small sliding door set into the wall.

"It's a dumbwaiter," Mallory said. "Servants used it to send trays of breakfast and stuff upstairs. There must be another door like this in one of the bedrooms."

"That thing sounds like it's in the shaft," Jared said.

Mallory leaned her whole body into the metal box. "It's too small for me. One of you is going to have to go."

Simon looked at her skeptically. "I don't know. What if the ropes aren't that good anymore?"

"It would just be a short fall," Mallory said, and both the boys looked at her in astonishment.

"Oh, fine, I'll go." Jared was pleased to find something Mallory couldn't do. She looked a little bit put out. Simon just looked worried.

The inside was dirty and it smelled like old wood. Jared folded his legs in and bent his head forward. He fit, but only barely.

"Is the squirrel-thing even still in the dumbwaiter shaft?" Simon's voice sounded tinny and distant.

"I don't know," Jared said softly, listening to the echoes of his words. "I don't hear anything."

Mallory pulled the rope. With a little jolt and some shaking, the dumbwaiter began to move Jared up inside the wall. "Can you see anything?"

"No," Jared called. He could hear the

scratching sound, but it was distant. "It's completely black."

Mallory winched the dumbwaiter back down. "There's got to be a light around here somewhere." She opened a few drawers until she found the stub of a white candle and a mason jar. Turning a knob on the stove, she lit the wick off one of the gas burners, dripped hot wax into the jar, and pressed the candle against it to hold it in place. "Here, Jared. Hold this."

"Mallory, I don't even hear the thing anymore," said Simon.

"Maybe it's hiding," said Mallory, and yanked on the rope.

Jared tried to tuck himself deeper into the dumbwaiter, but there was no room. He wanted to tell them that this was stupid and that he'd chickened out, but he said nothing. Instead, he let himself be raised into the darkness, holding the makeshift lantern.

The metal box went up a few feet inside the wall. The light from the candle was a small halo, reflecting things erratically. The squirrel-thing could have been right next to him, almost touching him, and he would not have noticed it.

"I don't see anything," he called down, but he wasn't sure if anyone heard him.

The ascent was slow. Jared felt like he couldn't breathe. His knees were pressing against his chest, and his feet were cramping from being bent so long. He wondered if the candle was sucking up all the available oxygen.

Then, with a jerk, the dumbwaiter stopped. Something scraped against the metal box.

"It won't go any farther," Mallory called up the chute. "Do you see anything?"

The dumbwaiter began to move.

Jared wasn't sure where he was.

"No," said Jared. "I think it's stuck."

There was more scraping now, as though something was trying to claw through the top of the dumbwaiter. Jared yelped and tried to pound from the inside, hoping to frighten it off.

Just as suddenly, the dumbwaiter slid up an extra few feet and came to a halt again, this time in a room dimly lit by moonlight from a single, small window.

Jared scrambled out of the box. "I made it! I'm upstairs."

The room had a low ceiling, and the walls were covered in bookshelves. Looking around, he realized there was no door.

All of a sudden, Jared wasn't sure where he was.

Jared looked around the room.

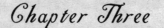

Chapter Three

IN WHICH There Are Many Riddles

Jared looked around the room. It was a smallish library, with one huge desk in the center. On it was an open book and a pair of old-fashioned, round glasses that caught the candlelight. Jared walked closer. The dim glow illuminated one title at a time as he scanned the shelves. They were all strange: *A Historie of Scottish Dwarves, A Compendium of Brownie Visitations from Around the World,* and *Anatomy of Insects and Other Flying Creatures.*

A collection of glass jars containing berries,

dried plants, and one filled with dull river stones sat at the edge of the desk. Nearby, a watercolor sketch showed a little girl and a man playing on the lawn. Jared's eyes fell on a note tossed on top of an open book, both coated in a thin layer of dust. The paper was yellowed with age, but handwritten on it was a strange little poem:

> *In a man's torso you will find*
> *My secret to all mankind*
> *If false and true can be the same*
> *You will soon know of my fame*
> *Up and up and up again*
> *Good luck dear friend*

He picked it up and read it through carefully. It was as though a message had been left here just for him. But by whom? What did the poem mean?

He heard a shout from downstairs. "Mallory! Simon! What are you doing up?"

Jared groaned. It just figured that Mom would get back from the store *now*.

"There was a squirrel in the wall," Jared could hear Mallory say.

Their mother cut her off. "Where's Jared?"

Neither of his siblings said anything.

"You bring that dumbwaiter down. If your brother is in there . . ."

Jared ran over in time to watch the box disappear down into the wall. His candle choked on wax and sputtered from his sudden movement, but it didn't go out.

"See?" Simon said weakly.

The dumbwaiter must have showed up, empty.

"Well, where is he then?"

"I don't know," Mallory said. "In bed, asleep?"

Their mother sighed. "Well, go on, both of you, and join him. Now!"

Jared listened to their retreating steps. They'd have to wait a while before they snuck back down to get him. That is, if they didn't just figure that the dumbwaiter had taken him all the way upstairs. They'd probably be surprised *not* to find him in bed. How could they know he was trapped in a room without a door?

There was a rustling behind him. Jared spun around. It came from the desk.

As he held up the makeshift lamp, Jared saw that something had been scrawled in the dust of the desk. Something that wasn't there before.

Click clack, watch your back.

Jared jumped, causing his candle to tilt. Running wax snuffed the flame. He stood in the darkness, so scared he could barely move. Something was here, in the room, and it could write!

He backed toward the empty chute, biting the inside of his lip to keep from screaming. He could hear the rustling of bags downstairs as his mother unpacked groceries.

"What are you?"

"What's there?" he whispered into the darkness. "What are you?"

Only silence answered him.

"I know you're there," Jared said.

But there was no reply and no more rustling.

Then he heard his mother on the stairs, a door, and nothing. Nothing but a silence so thick and heavy that it choked him. He felt that even breathing too loudly would give him away. Any moment the thing would be upon him.

There was a creak from inside the wall. Startled, Jared dropped the jar, then realized it was only the dumbwaiter. He felt his way through the darkness.

"Get in," his sister whispered up the shaft.

Jared squeezed into the metal box. He was so filled with relief that he barely noticed the ride down to the kitchen.

As soon as he got out, he started speaking.

"There was a library! A secret library with weird books. And something was in there—it wrote in the dust."

"*Shhhh*, Jared," Simon said. "Mom's going to hear us."

Jared held up the piece of paper with the poem on it. "Look at this. It has some kind of directions on it."

"Did you actually *see* anything?" Mallory asked.

"I saw the message in the dust. It said 'watch your back,'" Jared replied hotly.

Mallory shook her head. "That could have been written there ages ago."

"It wasn't," Jared insisted. "I saw the desk and there was nothing written there before."

"Calm down," Mallory said.

"Mallory, I saw it!"

Mallory grabbed his shirt in her fist. "Be quiet!"

"Mallory! Let go of your brother!" Their mother was standing at the top of the narrow kitchen stairs wearing a less-than-pleased expression. "I thought we already went through this. If I see any of you out of your beds, I am going to lock you in your rooms."

Mallory let go of Jared's shirt with a long glare.

"What if we need to go to the bathroom?" Simon asked.

"Just go to bed," their mother said.

When they got upstairs, Jared and Simon went off to their room. Jared pulled the covers over his head and scrunched his eyes shut.

"I believe you . . . about the note and all," Simon whispered, but Jared didn't reply. He was just glad to be in bed. He thought he could probably stay there for a whole week.

"Just chop it."

Clemency Pogue:
Fairy Killer

by JT PETTY
illustrated by WILL DAVIS

Clemency Pogue, upon finding herself attacked by a wicked fairy, remembers a lesson learned from Peter Pan. She shouts, "I don't believe in fairies," until the creature drops dead. After a mischievous hobgoblin arrives to tell Clem that she's killed six other fairies, Clem decides it's her duty to set the world aright. Clemency Pogue: Fairy Killer is the first book in Clem's hilarious adventures.

JT PETTY is a screenwriter and director. His film *Soft for Digging* was an Official Selection for the Sundance Film Festival. His film *Mimic: Sentinel* is in postproduction. This is his first book. He lives in Brooklyn, New York.

WILL DAVIS has an animation background, with experience working as a storyboard artist on television shows and commercials. This is the first book he has illustrated. Will lives in Pensacola, Florida.

Visit www.SimonSaysKids.com for more on *Clemency Pogue: Fairy Killer*.

Simon & Schuster Books for Young Readers
New York ✦ London ✦ Toronto ✦ Sydney

PROLOGUE

OF EVERYTHING there is good and bad. This is just how things work.

Ideas, dogs, smells, behavior, songs, guys, machines, cheeses, rabbits, shoes, friends, enemies, days, dreams, fairies; of all of these things and others, there are good and bad.

But rules cannot be viewed except by exceptions, and the exceptions are these: newborn mammals and bees. Newborn mammals are invariably good. Bees, however, are all bad.

CLEMENCY POGUE: FAIRY KILLER

If you are a bee sympathizer and find yourself insulted by the above remark, you can petition for the refund of the cost of this book. If this book was a gift and cost you nothing, the author will gladly refund you the love of the giver. If you paid for this book yourself and would like a refund, you may mail the author a self-addressed stamped envelope and a brief note explaining your case.

The author will promptly throw away everything but your address, which will be passed on to the authorities, in the hopes that they will detain you as a bee sympathizer, obviously insane, and in need of either treatment or imprisonment before you can do yourself or others harm.

CHAPTER 1

CLEMENCY POGUE was a child who listened to the stories she was told. It was a quality that saved her life once, and started her on a great adventure.

These stories were spun for Clem by her parents, who were good, kind, and creative people. Unfortunately they worked far away in the mansion of a very rich, very fancy man on the other side of the forest. In the gray of every morning they would march off to work, leaving Clem to her own devices until twilight time, when they would rush back home, her father carrying the evening's meal, her mother percolating with richly embellished stories distilled from the day's events.

"We met a polo player today with a face longer than his horse," she would say, or, "This afternoon the millionaire's nephew was pushed into a river by the lady he was courting. The young man was kidnapped by beavers and ended up as part of a dam. The millionaire is waiting until tomorrow to pull the boy out because the fishing on the other side of the dam is so good."

As Clem's mom unraveled these tales, her father would prepare the meal he had brought home, piling cornucopious gobs of savories and sweets onto the big wooden kitchen table. During dinner Clem would describe what discoveries and imaginations had occupied her day.

"Today," she would say, "I made cold sassafras tea that was sweeter than makes sense. So sweet, so sweet that when I left it alone, it was overwhelmed by its own sweetness. It bubbled and fizzed and could very well change the world."

After supper, from huge earthen mugs, they would drink steaming hot cider or tea or chocolate, and Clem's dad would sift through one of the many old and good stories he knew.

Her dad's stories were far too fantastic and sensible to have taken place in the world we take for granted. He told the old stories like Peter Pan and Wendy. He told stories that he made up as he went along like *The Epic of Gilbert and His Ambulatory Tub*. He told stories that were combinations of the two, mongrel tales like *The Tragi-Comic Blinding of Three Mice*.

The steam from her hot chocolate rising to tickle the cuddle of her chin, Clem sat listening to her dad:

" . . . and as soon as Wendy had spoken, Tinkerbell dropped dead. Dead as a gossamer-winged doorknob.

"'What have I done?' cried Wendy.

"'You've killed her, you brute!' said Peter. His shadow covered its eyes in horror.

"'But how?' she asked.

"'Why, you disbelieved her to death.' Peter explained, 'Fairies are strong, but such delicate things. Not too much more than intentions with wings.'"

Clemency listened, and a good thing, too.

CHAPTER 2

IN EARLY GRAY of the morning, Mr. and Mrs. Pogue marched off through the woods to work.

The sun crept upward sluggishly, fat and golden. As it just passed the horizon, setting aglow the tops of the trees but leaving the forest dark and secret below, Clemency walked out into the woods to begin the day's distractions. There would be no school until the leaves began to turn brown and the days began to shorten. That season was not so very far off, and Clem intended to make the most of her remaining vacation.

She held in her left hand a walking stick that she slung over her shoulder, with a basket hanging from the back end like a hobo's satchel. The basket was for the collection of sassafras roots; she intended to continue with her experiments in fizzing bubbly sweetness.

The walking stick was not for walking. Clem knew that there were places in the forest where danger lurked. And where it did not lurk, danger squatted, crouched, or lounged. There was one place where danger reclined, but Clemency usually avoided it. The walking stick she carried in case of danger, in case she came upon a wolf or a troll who needed to be shown what for.

Clem's pants rasped softly, *swst swst swst,* as her knees brushed with every stride. The pants were made of burlap and were a point of pride for Clemency. She had sewn them herself, and they were quite stylish. Unfortunately, the only fabric she could get her hands on was burlap, so they were a little rough around the seams.

The trees in the forest were as dark as cast iron, older than the dirt they grew in, fatter than walruses, and more twisted than yours truly. A carpet of moss covered the earth and climbed the trees, and was faintly luminous in the green light filtering down through the leaves.

Clem walked slowly about, following her nose toward the patches of sassafras saplings. The tingly, earthy smell led her farther and farther into the deep, dark woods, her path dotted with sassafras that she pulled from the soft earth, shook clean of dirt, and tossed over her shoulder into the basket.

As the sun approached its zenith, Clem

came to a great gorge that dropped abruptly from the edge of the trees. The ground just stopped at a rocky precipice, the exposed roots of ancient oaks dangling precariously into empty space.

Clem, tempter of fate and gravity, kicked a pebble over the edge and watched it tumble slowly down—a tiny white dot that grew tinier as it tumbled through space, falling and falling and falling for ages before tapping against the side of the gorge and bouncing out to tumble farther and farther still, before plunking into the lazy stream at the bottom.

Clem whistled in admiration of the gorge's depth. She felt the weight of her sassafras basket and decided it was about half as heavy as she could bear. She turned and started back home through the woods.

The moss underfoot had dried with the noon sun and crunched slightly as Clem wove her way through the trees. The woods were otherwise quiet. The slight crunch of moss underfoot, the swishing of her burlap pants, and a light rustle whenever Clem shifted her sassafras basket, but no more. Until a small waspish buzz entered Clem's ear for the briefest moment before a burning pinprick presented itself on her basket hand.

"Oh! Drat!" Clem dropped the walking stick and basket, sassafras spilling out aromatically. She looked at her hand, a tiny red dot midway between her thumb and pointer finger, a wasp's sting perhaps. But then another, near her elbow.

"Drat! Drat!" Clem swatted at the air by her elbow and saw the culprit, a tiny insect, slightly smaller than a wasp, the color of yam flesh. The insect descended onto her side and stung her again.

The otherwise peaceable Clem, thrice stung, lost her gentle disposition. She slapped the insect against her side mightily, with a gesture like a very fat man swarthily admiring his own girth.

The insect took no heed, and stung her again, by the navel. She slapped it again, with surely enough force to kill a cow, let alone this bug. Despite the blow, the tiny scoundrel stung her again on the arm.

Clem turned and ran. The insect pursued, diving between Clem's flailing arms and stinging her again several times. Clem stumbled over the giant roots of the ancient trees, calling out a forlorn "Drat!" with every sting.

Clem turned, focusing on the buzzing sound, and swatted at it. She batted the tiny aggressor against one of the great oaks. The tiny monster was stunned momentarily, and Clem turned again, falling over a root, but still moving, still running.

The great trees whirred past like locomotives. In the back of her head Clem could still faintly hear the buzzing. The little beast was on her again. She tried to run faster, but her legs had filled with lead, her lungs were white and frozen for lack of air.

Clem burst through a low hedge of shrubs and out onto the gorge. The exposed roots of the mighty trees dangled before her over the void.

"Oh." Clem was so tired. "Drat." She turned just in time to see the infinitesimal fire bug buzz right up to her face. In the brief instant before it stung her on the tip of the nose, Clem realized what the tiny creature was.

Its body was that of a human, tiny arms and legs, little fingers and toes like threads, a little person perfectly formed save for any bits that you could not show on television. It had a sweet-potato pallor, its skin the vibrant orange of cooked yams. From its back, four dragonfly wings whirred and buzzed like water spattering on a hot griddle.

The tiny aggressor was a fairy, and a mean one. In its hand it held a wand like a tiny cigarette, dull white all the way up with a searing orange tip, which it thrust into the end of Clemency's nose.

Clem swatted at the imp in a mad-ape rage. The fairy dodged backward with malicious grace, dove forward again and stung Clemency's cheek. Only an inch away from her eye, Clem could see the fairy grinning, bubbling over with her own evil.

Clem drew in a great bellowsful of air, shaped her lower lip like the spout of a pitcher, and puffed upward. The fairy was blown from her face, tumbling in midair. Clem raised her arms and brought her hands together in a clap that would easily have brained an elephant.

The fairy emerged from her hands unshaken, grinning like a barracuda. It was invincible. It dove forward at Clem's neck, and she fell backward, trying to evade the tiny burning barb.

She realized an important thing as her legs buckled and she fell backward. She realized that there would be no ground to catch her for the next thousand feet or so; she was falling into the gorge.

Clem's breath left her as the treetops arched away in a rush. Her arms pinwheeled backward. Straight as a board, she fell like a domino into the emptiness.

Hard wood smacked her in the back; the exposed roots of the mighty oaks dangling over the nothing caught and cradled her in their gnarled bark.

Clem was thankful for the roots, not for saving her so much as for delaying her doom. She knew there was no escape. Above her, she could see the whirring wings of the fairy glowing in the afternoon sun. It hovered, seeming to savor the anticipation of cutting off a girl's life after a scant ten years, just on the verge of a great discovery in cold sassafras technology. She knew the fairy would not let her back onto land, and she knew that all that awaited her in the other direction was the "Big Fall," followed by the "Big Splat." She imagined she would not be in any state to care when it came time for the "Big Getting Eaten by Ants." Even if she somehow managed to land in the stream at the gorge's bottom, it would only mean that she would end up soup instead of porridge.

And how could she fight? The fairy was indestructible, as had been amply demonstrated. But then again . . .

Clem, as I said, was a child who listened to the stories she was told. Balanced over her final resting place, and the "awfully big adventure" waiting for her when she fell, the story of Peter Pan and Wendy returned to her.

There was, in the story of the little boy who never grew up, instruction for the extermination of fairies. Clem, secret weapon on her tongue's tip, saw past the certainty of her own death.

She looked at the little yam-colored beast hovering above her and narrowed her eyes like a gunslinger.

"I don't believe in fairies," she said.

The fairy lurched backward and crossed its arms in front of its face. An uncertain, tense moment passed like a fart in a crowd, and then the barracuda grin returned to the fairy's angelic face. The little monster descended on dear Clem.

"I don't believe in fairies!" she said again. "I don't believe in fairies!"

The fairy landed gracefully on Clem's burlap pants and hopped upward toward her face.

"I don't believe in fairies! I don't believe in fairies!" Clem edged backward, trying to keep the fairy away from her face. The roots began to creak, as her weight leaned more heavily on their extremes.

"I don't believe in fairies!" Clem stopped edging and wrapped her fingers tightly around the roots below her. The fairy arrived at her neck, took its burning-hot wand in both hands and raised it above its head like an ax.

"I don't believe in fairies!" Clem shouted, her words tumbling down below her into the gorge.

The fairy's grin faltered. An expression crossed her face as if, despite scale, she had just swallowed a bug. She did a tiny pirouette, and dropped dead as a gossamer-winged doorknob, lying in the tiny hollow where Clem's neck and chest met.

Clem lay for a moment, trying to gather her thoughts, which had scattered like elephants from a mouse. A perilous creaking in the roots below her put an end to her ruminations, and very carefully she turned herself around so that she was facing the edge of the cliff. She gathered herself onto her hands and knees, and the fairy fell from its cradle at the base of her neck.

The tiny imp spiraled down into the gorge, a sunlit glint that flickered and twirled down slowly toward the rocks.

Clem crawled up the fattest root and onto the safety of the ground just as, near the edge of the woods, the ground, in a mighty soil geyser, exploded.

The Conch Bearer

by Chitra Banerjee Divakaruni

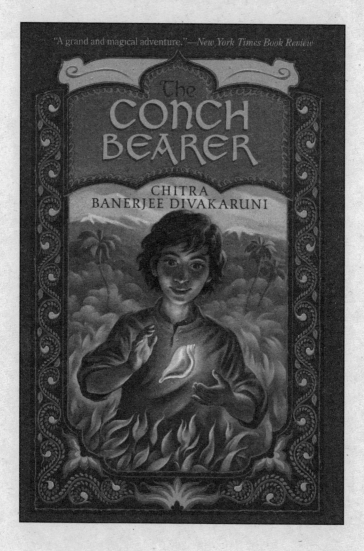

"A grand and magical adventure." —*New York Times Book Review*

The
CONCH
BEARER

CHITRA
BANERJEE DIVAKARUNI

Turn the page to be swept along the teeming streets of Kolkata and high into the Himilayas as twelve-year-old Anand faces a magical conch shell, the darkest forces of evil, and the most important journey of his life.

"A grand and magical adventure."
—*New York Times Book Review*

CHITRA BANERJEE DIVAKARUNI was born in India and currently lives in Texas, where she teaches creative writing at the University of Houston. She is the author of four adult novels, including the acclaimed *The Mistress of Spices*, *Sister of My Heart*, *The Vine of Desire*, and the newly published *The Queen of Dreams*; two short story collections, *Arranged Marriage* and *The Unknown Errors of Our Lives*; four volumes of poetry; and a novel for young readers, *Neela: Victory Song*. Her work has appeared in the *New Yorker*, *Atlantic Monthly*, and the *New York Times*.

Visit www.SimonSaysKids.com for more on *The Conch Bearer*, including a reading group guide.

Aladdin Paperbacks
New York ✦ London ✦ Toronto ✦ Sydney

THE NIGHT VISITOR

It was dark by the time Anand got off work, and he was very angry. Haru was supposed to let him go by 4 P.M., but he often found an excuse to keep Anand longer. Today he had claimed that Anand had not wiped the tables properly and made him do them all over again.

Anand had scrubbed the pocked wood of the tables furiously, biting his lip to make himself stay silent. Arguing, he knew, would only earn him a slap. Now he was going to be late for the market! Today was payday, and he had promised his mother that he would stop at the vegetable bazaar. For days now they'd had nothing to eat except potatoes and white radish boiled with rice, and he was tired of it. He had hoped to get a bunch of fresh, crisp spinach, or some sheem beans to fry up with chilies. But by now most of the pavement vendors would be gone. *If only I had the power to run my hands over the tables and make them new and shiny!* he thought. *But no, if I knew how to work that kind of changing magic, I'd start with Haru's black heart.*

Bone tired though he was, Anand ran all the way to the

vegetable market. Just as he had feared, the bazaar was deserted, the ground littered with wilted cabbage leaves and banana peels. Only the big stall with the neon lights, the one that charged extra for everything and had a big red sign that said NO BARGAINING, was still open. Anand walked up to it warily, knowing that most of the items there were beyond his budget. But maybe there would be something not so fresh. Then his eyes were caught by the pile of mangoes. Mangoes in winter! Where had the store-keeper found them? They were plump and soft and just the right ripeness, their skins a glowing orange streaked with red. How long had it been since Anand had eaten a mango? He swallowed, imagining the sweet juice that would fill his mouth when he took a big bite, and asked how much they were.

"Two rupees each," said the storekeeper in a bored voice. Obviously, he didn't think the ragged boy standing in front of him could afford the price.

Anand opened his mouth to protest. Why, the store-keeper was charging twice as much as what the pavement vendors would have charged! But he said nothing. The man would only shrug insolently and tell him to go else-where. He hesitated, then took out the meager bundle of rupee notes he had tucked into his waistband and peeled off two of them. He carefully picked the biggest, fattest mango, hefting it in his palm. Wouldn't Meera be amazed when he showed up with this beauty!

By now it was late and windier than ever, and Anand had to keep his head lowered to avoid the dust and debris flying through the air. Thankfully, he didn't feel cold. Why, he thought in surprise, he hadn't felt cold all day, not since he gave the old man his tea! He hoped the old man had found a place to shelter himself for the night. It looked like it was going to be a rough one.

The streets were strangely empty as Anand made his way home. Was it because it was dinnertime, or was it this unpleasant wind? The small businesses that lined the street—the printing presses and machine shops—had turned off their lights, padlocked their gates, and sent their employees home. With a brief pang of envy, Anand imagined them safe in their warm, lighted houses, listening to songs on the radio or sitting around a table, eating a hot meal, maybe a chicken curry with rice. After dinner the children would crowd around their father, begging for a story. The mother would bring bowls of sweet milk pudding from the kitchen. That was how it had been with his family, too, before . . . .

Anand shook his head to clear the memories. What use was it to long for what was no longer there? He'd better concentrate on getting home quickly. He'd have to start the cooking because Mother wouldn't be home until much later, and Meera couldn't be trusted to light the kerosene stove on her own. She couldn't do much of anything since the *bad-luck accident*, that's how he thought of it, had happened to her. He hoped she had remembered to wash the plates and fill the big earthen pitcher with water from the tenement's tube well. Sometimes when he came home, she would still be sitting on her bedding with a vacant look on her face, and he knew she hadn't moved from there since morning. But he never had the heart to scold her.

He passed the cigarette shop, surprised to see that it, too, was closed. Before today, no matter how late he had been in coming back from work, it had always been open, its shiny radio blaring hits from the latest Hindi movies. There was always a crowd of young men around it, joking and jostling around, smoking beedis or chewing on betel leaves and spitting out the red juice wherever they pleased. But today, with its shutters pulled down and locked, the shop looked abandoned and eerie, and Anand walked past it as quickly as he could.

Right around then he became aware that someone was following him. He wasn't sure how he knew it. There were no sounds—not that he would have heard footsteps in all this wind. Nor was there anyone behind him when he forced himself to whirl around and look. The street was empty and dark—a streetlight had burned out—and Anand realized that he was at the same crossing where Meera had been when the accident that had turned her strange and silent had occurred. He pushed the thought away from him with a shiver and quickened his steps. *There's no one behind me, no one*, he said to himself over and over, and, under that, *Mustn't fall, mustn't fall.* Because then, whatever was behind him would catch up.

There's no one behind me. Mustn't fall.

He was running now. There was a fog all around him, obscuring the shapes of the shacks and turning the alleys into unfamiliar, yawning tunnels. His foot caught on something, and he went sprawling. The mango fell from his hand and rolled into the darkness. Oh no! Not the mango he'd spent two whole hard-earned rupees on! He scrabbled desperately for it, but felt nothing but asphalt and dirt. He wanted to search more, but something told him it wasn't safe to delay any longer. Where had the fog come from, anyway? How could it be windy and foggy at the same time? Was this his street? Where was his house, then? He looked around wildly, not recognizing anything. *Help me!* He called inside his head, not knowing to whom he called. *Help!* He was ashamed to be acting this way, like a child. The fog in front of him thinned for a moment. Ah! There was his shack with its warped tin door! He had never been so happy to see it. He knocked frantically on the door, calling to Meera to open up, hurry, hurry. He heard her unsteady steps, then the bolt sliding across. He threw himself inside, slammed the door behind him, and bolted it again. He leaned his back against the door, his heart pounding. Meera stared at him, a startled look on her face.

He forced himself to smile because he didn't want to scare her. "Don't worry, Meera," he said, though his throat was so dry he could barely speak. "Everything's all right."

Then he heard the knocking. *Tap, tap, tong*. Someone was hitting the door with . . . a stick? a piece of metal? He could feel the vibration against his shoulder blades. He jumped away from the door and looked around for a weapon, something with which to defend himself and his sister. In the flickering light of the small oil lamp, he could see nothing except an old bonti, its blade dulled from years of cutting vegetables. Somehow he didn't think it would stop whoever was outside.

Then he heard the voice, deep and rusty, as if it had been at the bottom of a river for a long time.

"Anand," it said. "Let me in."

৩✬৩

Anand didn't know how long he stood in the middle of the room, eyes squinched shut, heart pounding madly. But the knocking didn't stop, as he had hoped. There it was again.

Tap, tap, tong.

"Go away," he whispered through dry lips.

"Let me in, Anand," the voice said. "I won't hurt you."

Right! Anand thought. That's what all the evil beings in his storybooks said, the monsters and witches, the daki-nis who drank blood.

"I don't believe you! I don't even know who you are!" he shouted. "Go away now, before I yell for the neigh-bors."

"Your neighbors won't come. They won't even hear

you over the wind. And even if they did, they'd be too scared, because of the killing—"

"How did you know about the . . . killing?" Anand asked, astonished, stumbling over the word. No one in the neighborhood spoke of it, not out loud like this, anyway. Like Anand, they all called it "the accident," as though renaming it could make it into something less dangerous.

The voice didn't answer his question. "In any case, you do know who I am," it said instead with a little laugh. "I'm the old man to whom you gave your tea."

Perhaps it was the laugh, or the memory of the old man's hand, light as a bird's foot in his hand, but Anand felt less scared. He wasn't completely convinced, though.

"Why did you follow me home?" he asked.

"Don't you know? You called for me—for us—and we came."

"I never called anyone," Anand said. Then he added, suspiciously, "What do you want from me?"

"Did you not call for help a little while ago?" the old man said.

"But that was in my head—"

"Exactly," said the man, a smile in his voice. "But you're right. I do want something. And in return I have something to offer you. But I can't discuss these things with a closed door between us. Please?"

Wondering if he was making a terrible mistake, Anand motioned to Meera to get behind him. *What if it's a trick?*

a voice inside him whispered. Ignoring it, he raised a trembling hand and unbolted the door. It was only when the door had creaked open on its hinges that he remembered that the man had said "*we* came."

But thank heavens, the old man was alone. Perhaps I misheard him, Anand thought. Something about him was different, though. Was it Anand's imagination, or did he seem straighter and taller? His white hair and beard glowed eerily in the dim light from the lamp as he stepped into the room, and there was a brightness in his eyes. The cloth bag was slung over his shoulder.

"Thank you," he said with a slight bow. "The wind was becoming rather unpleasant." As Anand watched, he walked to each corner of the room and made the same strange motion with his hand that Anand had seen him make earlier. Then he sat down on the mat the boy had spread out for him.

"It's very unusual for it to be so windy here," Anand said, mostly because he didn't know what else to say. He wondered if it had been the old man whom he had felt following him earlier. Somehow he didn't think so. The old man was strange, but Anand didn't feel scared when he looked at him. If anything, he felt happy. That was odd. Why should he feel happy looking at this ragged stranger whom he'd never met before today?

"I'm afraid I'm partly responsible for the wind," the old man was saying with a rueful grin.

"What do you mean? Did you . . . make . . . the wind happen?" As soon as he said it, Anand felt stupid. People didn't make winds happen.

But the old man didn't seem to think it was a stupid question. "I didn't," he replied. "Someone who wanted to stop me did. But before I explain things, is it possible to get a bite to eat? I'm starving. Only had a glass of tea all day, you know, and a few pooris!"

Anand jumped to his feet, embarrassed. "Of course! I'll start the rice and lentil stew right away. That's all we have, I'm afraid." He hunted around in the corner for the pot. Thankfully Meera had remembered to wash it today. He glanced at Meera, who was unusually quiet. She had crept close to the old man as he talked and was watching him intently. This surprised him. Ever since the killing, she'd been terrified of strangers, and on the few occasions when they had neighbors visiting them, she had curled up on her pallet in the far corner of the room, with the bedclothes drawn over her head.

Anand lit the stove, threw a few handfuls of rice and lentils into the pot, and added water, salt, turmeric, and chili powder. In twenty minutes, it would form a bubbly stew. Once again, he wished he'd been able to pick up a few vegetables. And that mango! If he hadn't dropped it, he could have cut each of them a slice to eat after dinner. He wanted to kick himself for being so clumsy.

The lamp in the corner flickered and the flame grew

small. Anand could tell it was running out of oil. He reached for the bottle to refill it, then remembered that it was empty. He'd been supposed to buy some oil, too, on his way home, but the wind and the fog and the fear had driven it out of his mind.

The lamp wavered and went out. Now there were only the blue flames from the kerosene stove.

"Maybe I can help," the old man said. He rummaged in his bag and came up with the stub of a candle. It wasn't much, Anand thought as he lighted it, but at least it would last through dinner.

"I've a couple of other things here that you may be able to use," the man said. He held up a small yellow squash and a handful of green beans, and Anand thankfully chopped them up and threw them into the pot. The room began to fill with a delicious smell. As though, Anand thought, he'd put lots of expensive spices into the pot. They sat in the small golden circle of light thrown out by the candle stub, waiting for the lentils to cook. As they waited, the old man told them his story.

THE SILVER VALLEY

"My story begins long before you or I were born," the old man said, "when this city that is called Kolkata today was a swamp where tigers roamed. It begins six thousand years ago in a hidden valley of the Himalayas—the Silver Valley, as it is called by those who know it. The Silver Valley! Even now it is the most beautiful place in the world, protected by the jagged, icy swords of the mountains that form a ring around it. Only a few people know the secret passes that lead into its fragrant groves and the shining lakes of clearest water from which it takes its name. Here, many ages ago, a group of men with special powers came together with the dream of perfecting those powers and using them to further goodness in the world. They called themselves the Brotherhood of Healers, and over the centuries they taught their powers to other young men who came to them, called or chosen from among many."

"What kinds of powers?" Anand asked, fascinated. He wasn't sure he believed what the old man was saying. It sounded a bit like the fairy tales his mother used to tell him when she had the time for such things. But he was happy to listen to any story that involved magic.

"Powers of the mind," the old man said. He put out his forefinger and touched Anand lightly in the center of his forehead. "There are worlds upon worlds of power in there, far beyond what you can imagine. The Healers knew how to draw upon them."

"What can the Healers do?"

"Some can look into the future and advise men and women of what to do, and what to avoid. Some can cure sicknesses of the body and mind. Some transport themselves to places thousands of miles away. Some travel through time to bygone ages. Some know special chants to create rain or storm—or wind and fog—"

"Like the wind and fog outside?"

The old man nodded. For a second his eyes shone golden in the candle's light. "Others can make riches fall from the sky. And once in a great while, a Healer will know how to use the conch."

The old man's words vibrated through the small room. They made the hairs on Anand's arms stand up.

"The conch!" He spoke slowly, savoring the sound of the words in his mouth. "What's that?"

"It came out of an ancient time, the time of myth, when, it is said, great heroes roamed the earth. These heroes were the sons of gods—and their fathers often gave them magical gifts. Two such heroes were named Nakul and Sahadev. Their fathers, the Ashwini Kumars, who were the physicians of the gods, gave them the conch. With it, Nakul and Sahadev could heal both men and animals and cure the land of famine and drought. At the great battle of Kuru Kshetra, it is said, they even used it to bring dead warriors back to life. But in doing this, they overstepped their bounds, and in punishment the conch was taken from them and buried deep in a valley of the Himalayas, for the gods felt that men were not ready for such a gift. For centuries it lay there, lost, while armies and factions warred across the land, killing and maiming and laying the earth bare." The old man paused.

"What happened then?"

"We don't know. The early part of the story is written in the Book of Heroes, but then the trail is lost. Perhaps, when time changed and the fourth age of man—the ink-dark Kali Yug that we now live in—began, it was time for the conch to be found again. Maybe it was a hill tribe, digging for roots, that discovered it. They would not have known how to use the conch, but they recognized it as an object of power. Maybe they brought it to a holy man, a sadhu meditating near the source of the Ganges. And perhaps he glimpsed a small part of its greatness and gave it to a favorite disciple, someone with the potential to use that greatness in the service of mankind. All we know for certain is that when the Brotherhood was started six thousand years ago, the conch was already present in the center of the Silver Valley, housed inside a crystal shrine. Around it the Healers built a meditation hall where they met each dawn. Though no one except the Keeper of the Conch was permitted to handle it, each Healer knew how sacred it was, and how potent. They knew that its presence alone made it possible for them to renew their own powers each day. They also knew that these powers were not theirs to use for selfish ends."

The stranger's face grew sorrowful, and he gazed at a spot above Anand's head as though there were images drawn in the shadows that only he could see.

"But once in a while there came a Healer who grew to covet the conch's power and wanted it for himself, to bring himself glory. In the past, when the Brotherhood was stronger and more attuned to one another, such a man would be discovered immediately and reprimanded. And if he did not see the wrongness of his desire and repent, he would be sent away, with a spell laid on him so that he could never return to the valley. But in Kali Yug, the time of disintegration and darkness, the Brotherhood was diminished, for many of the masters felt they were needed down in the plains, to ease the suffering of humanity by mingling among them. And perhaps we were not as careful of whom we admitted to the Brotherhood, for interest in the healing arts—and indeed the belief in them—had waned. We were badly in need of new students to whom the knowledge could be passed along. And that was how *he* came to us."

Here the old man paused as though he were listening to something. Anand, too, listened, but he could hear nothing but the wind.

"Who are you talking about?" he asked.

"His name is Surabhanu, though it is with reluctance that I name him for you. For in spite of the yantras, the protective runes I've drawn in the corners of the room, he is sure to hear the echo of his name and sense where I am. And in my present condition, I don't have enough power left to face him again."

Anand looked curiously at the old man. There were so many questions he yearned to ask. He wanted to know more about the valley, to which he was strangely drawn. In its loveliness, it seemed to him the exact opposite of this claustrophobic tenement that he hated so much. He wanted to learn more about the Brotherhood, too. It seemed to be a new and wonderful kind of family, one that spread its protective arms around you and never went away somewhere and left you behind.

But he chose the most urgent question. "Why does Sura—this man want to find you?" As he spoke, he had a strange feeling—almost as though a slimy tentacle had touched the back of his neck. He shuddered.

The old man gave him a shrewd glance. "You felt that, didn't you? That is the finger of his attention, sweeping this area of the city. In spite of the covering I've thrown over myself, he guesses I am somewhere here, in the tenements. And when we speak of him, even without saying his name, it creates a certain connection between us. But let me finish the story quickly—I fear time is running out.

"He came to us, enchanting us with his youth and beauty, the sweetness of his nature, and the passion with which he wanted to learn. We thought that in him we had found our next Keeper of the Conch, and this was important because our current Keeper was old, and ill with a wasting disease that made him suffer much. And so we gave the young man duties and responsibilities beyond what he was ready for. Perhaps our mistake began there. We allowed him to spend as much time with the conch as he wanted so that he could study its special qualities and learn how to invoke them. At what stage the dark changes in him began, I don't know. Already he had learned enough spells to hide them from us. Or perhaps we didn't see them because we wanted so desperately to believe in him. But slowly he began speaking to one or two of the Brotherhood—those who were dazzled by his charisma or who had a streak of darkness sleeping inside them. He told them that our powers were far greater than we realized, and that we were wasting them in this sleepy little valley. He said we had been foolish to vow to use our powers only to serve others. Why, together we could take over the entire earth and rule it with our wisdom! Would that not be a good thing? For

was the earth not in a sorry state, overcrowded with foolish or evil men and women who needed to be subdued and
guided? Then the Golden Age might return again."

The old man sighed. "Ah, yes, he was clever enough to
promise them goodness, and a return of Satya Yug, the
first age, age of truth. He spoke so persuasively that most
of them did not remember that goodness does not covet
power or break the vows it has made.

"But one or two of the Healers he had misjudged. And
they spoke to some others, and they to more, until he was
called before the council, who questioned him. After much
debate, it was decided that he must leave the Brotherhood
the next day, and he, seeming to understand his error,
agreed to do so. But he disappeared that very night, breaking through our shields—and with him he took the conch!
In the morning when we came together to meditate, we
found the crystal shrine cracked and empty. And worse—
the old Keeper, who must have tried to stop him, was
sprawled across the threshold of the hall, dead."

The old man gazed at the floor, silent, until it seemed to
Anand that he had forgotten where he was.

Anand was reluctant to disturb him in his sorrow. But
he, too, now had the feeling that time was running out.

"And then?" he urged.

"The council knew that without the conch, the
Brotherhood would soon crumble. Already we were for-
getting the chants and gestures of power, and when we

tried to send our vision over the earth, we saw only patches of gray. More importantly, they knew that in the thief's hands the conch would be gravely dangerous. If he learned how to use it to its utmost capacity, he would unleash disaster across all the worlds, the seen and the unseen. So the Chief Healer summoned the senior-most of the masters—there were eight of us—and sent us, in pairs, to search the four directions.

"My partner and I were sent south. I would need many hours to tell you how long we traveled and how hard we searched, and how, finally, we found the thief, disguised as he was. Or with what difficulty we entered his domain, eluded his followers, and stole away the conch—for with the conch in his possession, we dared not challenge him to a battle. Enough to say that now I have the conch with me, and my task—an urgent one—is to return it to its proper place."

"But where's your partner?" Anand couldn't help asking.

"Dead." The old man's voice was heavy. "He sacrificed himself, staying back to battle the thief so that I could escape with the conch. He was like my brother—we had come to the Silver Valley in the same year, and had trained together—" His eyes blazed for a moment. To Anand they looked white, like metal that is very hot. Then the old man lowered his head. "I can't squander my powers—reduced as they are now—on thoughts of sorrow or revenge. I must stay focused on my task. But to succeed, I need your help."

"*My* help!" Anand's voice was squeaky with disbelief. "How can *I* help you?"

"I need an assistant, someone to journey with me. To protect my back, as it were. There are things I'm not able to do that you might be able to do for me. Places you might be able to enter. And if there comes a time when the thief does catch up with me, you might be able to get away with the conch. Because no one would expect a mere boy to be the Conch Bearer."

Conch Bearer! The words resonated inside Anand like peals from a distant bell. More than anything else, he wanted to accept the old man's offer. But was he—the boy whom Haru yelled at every day for being slow and stupid, whom passing schoolchildren laughed at because of his torn, mismatched clothes—good enough to be a Master Healer's assistant?

"Why did you choose me?" he stammered. "I don't have any special powers. How can I help you stop the conch thief, or protect you from him?"

"I don't expect you to do that. Even I, trained as I am, couldn't do it for my brother Healer, could I? But I was called to you because of your belief in magic—and your desire to enter its secret domain."

"You heard my wish?" Anand asked incredulously. "But how—"

"At another time, I will explain all, my curious young man! For now, let me just say, yes, I heard. But more importantly, the conch seemed to hear, too. I could sense it turning its attention to you. Who knows? Maybe it sensed in you a special gift that neither you nor I know of yet. And when you touched my hand earlier today, giving me the tea, I felt your kindness. That itself is a valuable gift."

"Do you really think so?" Anand asked hesitantly. He still didn't feel valuable in any way.

The old man nodded. Then he added, "Will you come with me?"

THE FARSALA TRILOGY

BOOK I
FALL OF A KINGDOM

by HILARI BELL

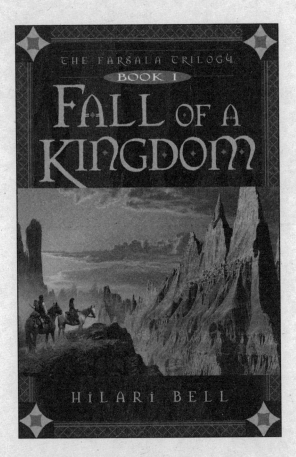

Who was Sorahb?

Stories tell of a hero who will come to Farsala's aid when the need is greatest. Now that time has come. Read an excerpt from the first book in the celebrated trilogy that Tamora Pierce called "[A]n amazing tale of adventure, fear, magic, conquest, and rebellion!"

HILARI BELL has written several science fiction and fantasy books for young readers, including *Songs of Power* and *A Matter of Profit*. She lives in Denver, Colorado.

For more information about The Farsala Trilogy, visit www.SimonSaysTEEN.com.

Simon Pulse
New York ✦ London ✦ Toronto ✦ Sydney

OUTSIDE OF HIS ORIGINS *in the time of ancient legends, little is known of Sorahb. We know that he was a brilliant military commander, a shrewd ruler, and a mighty sorcerer—but how can a man so young have been all of these things? Was he a noble deghan? A peasant? Even, as some speculate, a Suud sorcerer in disguise? All this has been claimed, and more, but the one thing all agree upon is that he was a great hero, greater even than his father, Rostam. At least, if the legends are to be believed. . . .*

CHAPTER ONE

JIAAN

JIAAN DUCKED, and a bronze cup shaped like a ram's horn crashed into the wall behind him. It didn't clatter on the floor, since the thick carpets that had already absorbed its contents muffled the sound. He hoped the carpets wouldn't be too hard to clean. Jiaan knew that some people found it harder than others to fight off the djinn of rage. But he didn't think the lady Soraya was even trying.

"Lady, if you'll just lis—"

"I *have* listened," the girl snarled. Her grip tightened on the second cup. Her loose hair—the straight, black hair of the noblest of noble lines—was disheveled. The tight vest she wore beneath her loose, silk overrobe rose and fell with the force of her breathing. At fifteen, she was probably the most beautifully feminine creature

Jiaan had ever seen—so what djinn-cursed fool had taught her to throw like a shepherd boy?

"I have listened," she repeated. "But all I've heard is that my father—my own father!—seeks to cast me out like some peas—like broken rubbish!"

Like some peasant-spawned bastard. It was an insult so familiar that Jiaan's heart hardly flinched. At least she hadn't said it aloud. That surprised him; most deghasses wouldn't have given a moment's thought to the possibility that he might be offended. But Jiaan's father hadn't cast him out. Far from it. And High Commander Merahb didn't intend . . .

"He doesn't intend to cast you out." Jiaan made his tone reasonable, despite the way her lovely, dark eyes narrowed. "He only means to hide you away for a time, in order to—"

"Away in some peasant sty . . ."

The second cup flew, and Jiaan sidestepped nimbly.

". . . in some dung-sucking outland while . . ."

Her groping hand found a niche, carved into the outer wall between the arched windows, and came to rest on a goblet whose glass bowl glowed as blue as the heart of a flame. Its base was chased in gold. Its worth was probably ten times that of Jiaan's sword, and his sword was more costly than all his other possessions put together.

The goblet hurtled toward the wall. Jiaan leaped, cursing the carpets that hindered his feet. He caught the goblet with the tips of his fingers, fumbled with it for an endless moment, and settled it into a secure grasp.

The plate it had rested on, thrown like a discus, struck him full in the chest, bruising him even through the padded silk layers of his armor.

"Ow!" Had she distracted him deliberately? "He's only trying to save your life, you . . . Lady Soraya. The gahn rules all of Farsala. Even the high commander has to obey him."

"Dung!" she shrieked. The incense burner her hand fell on next—small but solid stone and bronze—made a dent in the heavy panels of the door at Jiaan's back. "The armies of Farsala haven't propitiated the war djinn since Rostam cast down the last djinn emperor. Centuries ago! And he thinks he's going to exile me for however long it takes to win his stupid war? Well, I won't—"

The door behind Jiaan opened. "You won't have any choice," said a woman's voice coldly. "And if you're overheard by the wrong people, your choices will become fewer—and even less pleasant than exile."

Jiaan stepped aside and bowed, the goblet still in his hands. Commander Merahb's wife, the lady Sudaba, moved gracefully into the small solarium.

Soraya froze, her hand clenched around the carved wooden

horse she'd been about to throw. "Madam my mother, have you heard of this . . . this outrage? What about my marr—"

"I imagine everyone has heard." Sudaba took the goblet from Jiaan and crossed the room to return it to its shelf. "But I see no reason to give them any more information about our family's private affairs." Her ironic gaze rested on Jiaan.

He bowed himself out of the room, but not before Sudaba seized her daughter's ear and twisted it.

His own peasant-born mother had twisted his ears, and paddled his buttocks as well. But along with occasional—and usually deserved—punishment, there had been warmth, laughter, and love. Not only from her, but even from the farmholder to whom Jiaan's father had given her, when he was required to wed a deghass and produce a noble heir. His mother had died of a fever two years after the commander had outraged everyone by taking a peasant-born bastard into his household as a page, instead of as a servant. Jiaan still missed her.

Jiaan looked around the second-story gallery on which he stood. Intricately carved rails, sanded, waxed, and polished, encircled the courtyard below. Summer was ending; the leaves on the ornamental bushes looked dusty, almost ready to turn and fall, but a handful of late roses still bloomed, and the splash of the fountain calmed his ruffled nerves.

The home in which he'd lived till he turned ten had rough, log walls, and the plain, plank floors had never seen a carpet—yet he thought he'd been luckier than the lady Soraya.

On the other hand, all she had to do was go quietly and be patient for a while. Was that too much to ask?

The door behind him opened, and Sudaba emerged. "Soraya will depart with you tomorrow morning," she said calmly.

"Yes, madam." Jiaan bowed. She was eight inches shorter than he, but the assurance in her eyes made him feel as if he were the smaller.

"You should have pointed out that her father is plotting to save her," Sudaba murmured. "At some risk."

The crash of priceless glass against the door made Jiaan wince.

Sudaba didn't even twitch. "And however inconvenient it may seem, it's much better than the alternative."

In fact, Jiaan had pointed out all those things. Soraya hadn't cared. "Yes, madam."

"This is just a ploy." Sudaba leaned on the gallery rail, gazing down at the garden with unseeing eyes. "Another move in the game. But a good one."

Jiaan settled back to wait with the ease of long practice, till she noticed his existence long enough to dismiss him. The late-afternoon sun lit the expensive, brocaded silk of her overrobe and the almost equally expensive, fine-woven linen underrobe beneath it. Gold on brown, to honor the approaching harvest. Her hair, as straight and black as her daughter's, was caught up in a complex coil, twined with silk ribbons knotted with glowing glass beads and the hawk feathers only a deghass, a lady of the noble class, could wear.

Jiaan's hair was brown and curly, like his mother's . . . and his father's. Many of the deghans had peasant hair. But not Sudaba. In her youth, the poets had said, she'd been as lovely and imperial as the moon. *And as distant,* Jiaan thought now, watching her calculate the political implications of her daughter's fate. *As indifferent.*

But then a black-haired boy, his brown skin as naked as the day, burst shrieking into the courtyard and toddled toward the fountain. Two nursemaids, armed with trousers and tunic, hurried after him.

Sudaba's frown faded and her eyes lit, her face suddenly, warmly maternal. Merdas, the long-awaited heir, had finally confirmed her status, eliminating the danger that she could be set aside allowing High Commander Merahb to take another wife. But still . . . Jiaan had served in the high commander's household for seven years—as page, as squire, and now as the commander's aide—and he had never seen Sudaba's face soften like that for Soraya.

On the other hand, her father loved her best. "The commander of the army must sacrifice the being he holds most precious in all the world," the priests had said. "Or the djinn of war will give their favor to the armies of the Hrum, who will roll over Farsala like the darkness of the pit itself."

Jiaan wondered uneasily which of the commander's enemies had bribed the priests to say it. And why. No, he didn't envy his half sister. Even if she was a silly, spoiled she-bitch.

CHAPTER TWO

SORAYA

ORAYA WENT ALONE down the stairs to the courtyard. The sun still crouched below the horizon, though the sky to the east was bright with its approach. It was light enough for her to see small puffs of steam when she breathed out. The cold weather was coming; rain, mud, and chills, and she was to be imprisoned in some sty in the outlands? She was fifteen this year—it was time for her to wed! She shivered.

She'd snarled at the maids who had awakened her to dress by candlelight, but she hadn't dared to refuse them, for behind the mouse-timid maids loomed her mother's shadow—and Sudaba was anything but timid. But it wasn't fear of Sudaba that was making her go. Not really.

Soraya crossed the garden and stalked down the stone-flagged walkway that passed under the servants' wing and out to the stables. Her escort waited there, his horse already saddled, his face pale in the gray light. Two of her father's armsmen, in the black-and-gold tunics of the House of the Leopard, accompanied him—not that all of them together could take her anywhere she didn't choose to go. Especially when she was on horseback. Jiaan smiled tentatively. Soraya scowled and turned away. She wasn't going because of him, and it probably wasn't fair to blame him for being the bearer of bad news, but she didn't feel like being fair. Particularly to the peasant-born bastard her foolish father had insisted on bringing into his household as a page, then as his aide, just as if he were a noble-born second son or an impoverished cousin.

One of the mousy maids brought up Soraya's pack, to be added to the load the mules carried. She waited while the grooms fussed with the ropes, trying to exude regal dignity and not shiver. If she looked regal enough, the servants, at least, might be fooled into thinking the whole thing was her idea.

Small bare feet made no sound on the stone floor, but Soraya caught a glimpse of the blue-striped nightdress, and she abandoned dignity to swoop down on Merdas just before he darted behind one of the horse's heels. It wasn't a charger, but even a placid horse might kick if startled.

"Merdas, don't run behind horses! You know better than that."

He squirmed in her arms to face her, warm and toddler-firm, pouting, because he really did know better. But Merdas never believed any horse would hurt him. Her brother. Her father's son.

"Djinn did it," he pronounced. At his age she had claimed the same. "Raya, horse!"

The nursery window overlooked the stable yard—he must have heard the hoofbeats. He had ears like a lynx where horses were concerned. And if there was a djinn who governed slipping past one's nurses, Merdas had it firmly under his control.

"I can't take you riding today, imp," said Soraya regretfully. "I'm going a long, long way. You'd get tired."

"Horse," said Merdas, who didn't believe he could get tired, either. Sometimes Soraya agreed with him.

"Sorry, no horse today. But if you're good, I'll bring you a present when I come back. How about that?"

The dark eyes turned thoughtful. Merdas liked presents, but . . . "Horse!" He squirmed again, kicking her in the stomach.

Where were his nurses? She could hand him over to the grooms, but she hated the thought of riding off with him howling behind her. "Horse, horse, horse!"

"I'll take him." It was Sudaba's voice.

Soraya spun, astonished. Her mother returned her gaze calmly, every braid in place, as if she always rose at dawn. She was dressed for riding, a modest split skirt beneath her overrobe—unlike Soraya.

"I didn't realize you were coming with me, madam." Soraya transferred Merdas into her outstretched arms, and he settled on her hip, reaching for the feathers in her hair. But for once he didn't have Sudaba's full attention. Her lips tightened as she took in the baggy men's trousers Soraya wore for riding. Not ladylike. Not proper for a deghass.

But making a scene in front of the servants wasn't proper either. "I thought it best to accompany you, daughter, in this difficult time."

To support Soraya in her troubles? No, to make certain her orders were obeyed. As if Soraya were an infant. Soraya scowled, but there was nothing she could do. The jumped-up page boy, Jiaan, looked startled, but Sudaba would care even less for his wishes than her daughter's.

Sudaba's maids brought out her baggage—far more than Soraya had brought—and several more mules were added to the caravan. Merdas' nurses scurried out and took him from his mother's arms.

"We're ready to depart, madam," Jiaan told Sudaba respectfully. He didn't even look at Soraya.

Sudaba mounted and set off, the armsmen trotting after her. But Soraya went to Merdas and covered his face with big, smacking kisses that made him giggle.

"A present when I come back," she promised, and then turned swiftly to her mare. The groom's cupped hands caught her bent knee and tossed her expertly up into the saddle. Soraya wrapped her legs around the mare's broad barrel and took her out without a backward glance. More regal that way. For if she looked back and Merdas reached for her, she might weep. And if he was indifferent to her departure—a perfectly normal reaction for a toddler, who had no idea how long she might be gone—she'd feel cheated. Besides . . .

She snickered, and Jiaan, who was trotting up beside her, stared, his annoyed scowl fading into curiosity.

If he'd been impertinent enough to ask why she laughed, she wouldn't have said anything, but he just watched her and let the silence stretch. And he looked almost embarrassingly like her father.

"I was just thinking that any grief Merdas showed would have been for his vanishing horseback ride, not for me."

Jiaan grinned, but his pale, greenish eyes—lighter than her father's, his peasant blood showed in that—were full of speculation.

Soraya knew what he was thinking. She'd heard it for almost two years—whispers in shadowy stalls, in the bushes in the courtyard, behind her back: "She really loves the boy. Or seems to. How can she when her mother . . ."

But Merdas couldn't take away affection that Sudaba had never given her in the first place. If anything, she'd come to understand her mother better since Merdas had been born, for the need to be mistress of her own house, to be the first woman in it, had been setting its heels to Soraya's sides lately as well. And her father's recent letters had hinted that marriage, a fine marriage, was under consideration. So what was this ridiculous sacrifice business? Certainly the priests demanded sacrifices of gold, but the sacrifice of life, of blood, hadn't been demanded since the days folk truly believed in the power of the djinn. Soraya sighed. She had to discuss this with her father. Sudaba needn't have worried that she'd rebel; in fact, Soraya would have gone even if her mother had forbidden it. This was the first important thing her father had asked of her.

THEY TOOK THE ROAD that followed Little Jamshid Creek, which flowed eventually into the Jamshid River. Sudaba rode at the head of the party, as a high-ranking deghass should. Soraya kept her horse back, but she maintained her dignified silence, answering Jiaan's occasional conversational attempts politely but not expanding on them. He soon gave up and stopped talking.

That suited Soraya. It was almost a full day's ride before the farms of the first village disrupted the sweeping plains of her father's estate, and silence was the proper greeting for windswept grass and the huge, open sky.

At dusk they began to encounter the kind of fields you weren't supposed to ride over—though sometimes, in the heat of the hunt, you did. When that happened, her father would send a groom to find the farmholder, with a small purse of copper stallions or a few silver falcons to set it right, but Soraya knew most deghans wouldn't bother to do the same. You had to eat, of course, but most deghans regarded plowed land as a waste of good pasture.

The inn at the small village was crude, but Soraya had stayed there before, and she knew it was clean and had a decent bathhouse. She frequently accompanied her parents on the six-day journey to Setesafon. It was Farsala's capital city, because the gahn's palace was there.

Soraya tossed her reins to the groom and slid off her horse. It had been a long ride, even for someone accustomed to the saddle. The innkeeper was already bowing Sudaba through the door. Soraya followed, waving over the first maid she saw to command a bath. Her escort would pay the tab.

AROUND MIDDAY THE HORSES picked their way down the shallow cliffs that separated the upland plains from the near-solid farm-lands—the flatter, wetter country where the lesser noble houses held land.

Then a short canter across country brought them to the Great Trade Road. No matter how many times she'd seen it, the wide, dusty tracks always intrigued Soraya. The carters who drove it tried to move their carts around, to keep any one set of ruts from becoming too deep, but after a while they deepened anyway, and the road shifted a bit to the north or south to make new tracks. Over the centuries it had become not one road, but dozens of twining trails, weaving their way from the Sendar Wall at the western border of Farsala to the invisible line in the east where the border deghans held back the Kadeshi.

Some of the laden carts on this road had come from even farther away, carrying second-rate steel and mechanical creations from the Iron Empire of the Hrum, to trade for glass, spices, and dyes from the savage lands of Kadesh, for even the Hrum's second-rate steel was better than anything the Kadeshi could produce. Some traders from both directions stopped in Farsala to trade for Farsalan silk, which was so strong that armor could be made from its gathered layers, like the padded tunic Jiaan was wearing—armor both stronger and lighter than the leather armor most folk used. Sometimes they traded for horses, too. Farsala's horses were the finest in the world, and even the culls from their herds were worth much in other lands.

Traders liked Farsala, Soraya's father said, and paid their travel tax willingly because the deghans kept the road free of bandits. Soraya had never met anyone willing to pay taxes, but the traders were a cheerful lot, calling out greetings and talking of the lands they'd visited as you rode beside their carts—though they wouldn't unwrap the mysterious bundles and crates of their loads unless you had coin in hand and were interested in buying more than a trinket or two.

On past trips Soraya had talked to the traders for candlemarks, to her father's amusement and her mother's disapproval. Sudaba would never permit casual conversation with such low-born men on this journey, just as Soraya's trousers had been taken away by her mother's maid and replaced with the voluminous, awkward split skirt.

Soraya sighed again. When she married, she would choose a man who let her wear what she pleased and talk to whomever she wished, like her father did. When she was married . . .

THE WEATHER HELD GOOD for two more days. The harvest was beginning, the fields full of peasants in their vulgar, brightly dyed clothes. Even little ones, barely older than Merdas, were fetching empty baskets for their elders or chasing off the birds. But midafternoon, on the fourth day of their journey, the clouds to the south began to build and darken.

Jiaan scowled at them—her father's scowl—the rising wind ruffling his curly, peasant hair, and he asked Sudaba if they could stop at the next village.

Soraya bit back the urge to argue. She might love a thunderstorm, but she knew the horses wouldn't.

So it came about that Soraya found herself, in the late afternoon, with time and energy to spare, cooped up in a bedchamber that was too small even to pace in. There were peasant designs painted on the furniture, and the painted shutters of the single, small window opened onto the inn's kitchen yard. The trees on the other side of the yard's wall rustled in the wind, their upper branches beginning to toss; but the window faced north, so that was all of the storm she could see.

At home Soraya had a south-facing room. She could sit at her open window, blanket wrapped around her, and watch the winter rains rush in, spitting lightning and growling like a lion, as the wind clawed at her hair. Sometimes she didn't close the shutters when the first drops struck her face. Sometimes she even went out in the storms. . . .

There was a shed roof not four feet below the windowsill. *Why not?* Her mother's maids had only taken away *one* pair of trousers.

Soraya pulled her next pair from inside one of her shifts, where she'd concealed them on the first night of the journey. She pinned her overrobe tight, grateful that it was split up the back for riding. It was the work of moments to swing one leg over the sill and pick her way down the shed's roof, rope-soled riding boots secure on the rough slats. Off to one side was a wood bin, conveniently placed for a girl who wasn't tall to reach with one toe and then wobble down to the ground.

Soraya grinned at the startled cook, who'd stopped pulling loaves from the oven under the shed's roof to stare at the source of the overhead footsteps. Then she turned and made for the gate that would lead to the inn's garden and, hopefully, to some open place where she could watch the storm come in.

PENDRAGON

BOOK SIX:
THE RIVERS OF ZADAA

by D. J. MacHale

In the breathtaking continuation of this *New York Times* bestselling series, Bobby's quest to save Halla from Saint Dane's evil influence takes him to Zadaa, where he joins forces with the Traveler Loor. In his quest to thwart Saint Dane's efforts to destroy Zadaa, Bobby realizes he holds the ultimate power.

D. J. MACHALE is a writer, director, and producer of several popular television series and movies that include *29 Down*; *Are You Afraid of the Dark?*; *Encyclopedia Brown, Boy Detective*; *Tower of Terror*; and *Ghostwriter*. Pendragon, his first book series, became an instant hit that included a *New York Times* bestseller. He lives in Southern California with his wife, Evangeline; his daughter, Keaton; a golden retriever, Maggie; and a kitten, Kaboodle.

Please visit www.thependragonadventure.com or www.SimonSaysKids.com to discover more about the Pendragon series.

Simon & Schuster Books for Young Readers
New York ✦ London ✦ Toronto ✦ Sydney

ZAÐAA

It began with a battle.

A nasty one. Then again, is there such a thing as a nice battle? I guess this one seemed especially vicious because it was over something so trivial. At least that's what I thought at the time. At stake was a couple gallons of water. I'm serious. Regular old everyday water. Not exactly the kind of thing you'd expect a group of professional warriors to fight to the death over, but that's not the way it works here on the territory of Zadaa. Water here is more valuable than food, more valuable than treasure. It's even more valuable than life. I know. I've seen people risk theirs to get a few precious drops.

How messed up is that?

Mark, Courtney, it's been a while since I've written a journal to you guys, and for that I apologize. I think after I tell you all that's happened since my last journal, you'll understand why. From the time I arrived here on Zadaa, I haven't had much time to think, let alone kick back and write. I'm doing it now because I'm about to set out on an adventure that was long in coming. I've tried to avoid it, but now I have no choice. Starting tomorrow, life is going to be very different for me. I feel as if I'm closing the first chapter on my life as a Traveler and beginning a new and more dangerous one. I know, that doesn't seem possible, but it's the truth. Before I tell you about it, I need to let you know what happened since I landed back on Zadaa. You'll need to hear it all to understand why I've chosen the path I'm about to take. Maybe writing it down will help me understand it a little better myself.

You won't be surprised to hear that Saint Dane is here. I've already run into him. It wasn't pretty. But more about that later. I also have a good idea of what the turning point is here on Zadaa. I think it has something to do with water . . . or the lack of it. I've no doubt that Saint Dane's evil plan for this territory is somehow tied in to the water trouble they're having. Bottom line is, our quest to stop Saint Dane's plan to crush all of Halla has come to Zadaa. This is our next challenge. And so we go.

I first want to tell you about the battle that happened soon after I arrived. It's important to hear because in many ways it's a small example of the bigger trouble I found on this territory. That, and because one of the warriors involved in the fight was my friend. Loor. The Traveler from Zadaa.

"Keep to yourself, Pendragon," Loor ordered as we strode along the dusty street of Xhaxhu city. "Stay in the shadows. Do not look anyone in the eye. It is dangerous for a Rokador to be seen in the city."

"But I'm not a Rokador," I complained.

"Do not argue," Loor said sharply. "Do as I say."

I didn't argue. I knew what she meant. There were two tribes living in this area of Zadaa. The Batu lived above ground in the cities. They were a dark-skinned race, made so because they lived for generations under the hot, desert sun. Loor was a Batu. The other tribe was the Rokador. They lived underground in a labyrinth of tunnels that spread through-out Zadaa. They weren't moles or anything; they were defi-nitely civilized. But as you might guess, living underground didn't do much for their tans. The Rokador were a light-skinned race. So with my white skin and light brown hair, I pretty much looked like a Rokador. And since there was some serious bad blood between the Batu and the Rokador, making myself invisible up here on the surface was a smart idea. To that end, Loor had me wearing heavy, dark clothing that cov-ered my head and arms. It was great for a disguise, not so great for keeping cool. I'm guesstimating that the tempera-ture in Xhaxhu averages about ninety degrees. On a cool day. So I was sweating like a fiend. Or at least a fiend in a sauna wearing a winter coat.

"Can't somebody take your place?" I asked. "I mean, we have more important things to worry about."

Loor looked straight ahead as she strode along. Her jaw set. I'd seen this look before. She had her game face on. I know you guys can picture her. She's hard to forget. I'd grown a few inches since I first met her on Denduron, but she still had me by a solid two inches. Her once almost-waist-length black hair was a bit shorter now, falling to her shoulders. I guess the long hair got in the way when she did her training. As you know, Loor is a warrior. Here on Zadaa they call the warrior class "Ghee." When I first met Loor, she was a warrior-in-training. Since then, she has been elevated to full-fledged warrior sta-tus. I'm guessing she was at the head of her class. She's that good. She even looks the part. This girl is totally cut. I'm talk-ing stupid-low body fat. It isn't hard to see this since her light-weight leather armor reveals a lot of skin. Wearing heavy metal armor like the knights of the Round Table wouldn't fly here on searing-hot Zadaa. You'd end up cooking like Spam in the can. Assuming Spam is actually cooked, which I'm not so sure about. But whatever. You get the idea. The warriors here had to be protected, but cool. Unlike me, who had to be wearing a wool-freakin'-blanket.

The muscles in her long arms and legs flexed as she moved down the street, making her look even more formidable. I guess when you're a professional warrior, having an awesome athletic body goes with the territory. So to speak.

"I have no choice but to fight today," Loor finally answered. "I am next in the rotation."

"Rotation?" I snapped. "What are you, a baseball pitcher? Have them change the schedule. Find a relief pitcher. If something happens to you then—"

"If I do not fight," Loor interrupted, "the Ghee commanders will mark me as a coward and banish me to a labor colony in the desert. Or I could get lucky and they would execute me."

"Oh," I said soberly. "Not a lot of wiggle room."

"Do not worry, Pendragon," she said, finally looking at me. "Our destiny is to stop Saint Dane. I will not let anything stand in our way."

I believed her, but that didn't mean I wasn't going to worry.

"Loor!" came a voice from behind us. Running to catch up was Saangi. I'm not exactly sure what her official title is, but I guess on Second Earth you would call her Loor's squire. You know, one of those young servants who are assigned to knights to take care of their every need. The Ghee warriors of Zadaa operated pretty much like the knights of old, without the Spam-can suits.

"You forgot this!" Saangi said, out of breath. She handed Loor a small, leather container that was about the size of a canteen. In fact that's exactly what it was, a canteen full of water.

"No," Loor said sternly. "I cannot use this."

"But you will need water if the battle is difficult—," Saangi protested.

"Take it back to my home," Loor said firmly. "And do not let anyone see you with it."

When Loor spoke in that serious tone, you didn't mess with her. At least I didn't. I figured Saangi knew better too. The girl's shoulders fell in disappointment. I'm guessing she was around fourteen, only a few years younger than me. She had the dark skin of the Batu, but unlike Loor, her hair was cut tight to her head, like a guy. She wore simple, dark clothes that looked sort of like Loor's, but they were made of cloth rather than leather. Someday she would wear the armor of a Ghee warrior, but until then, her job was to take care of Loor.

Oh yeah, one other thing. Saangi had another job. She was Loor's acolyte. She knew all about the Travelers and our mission to stop Saint Dane. I thought Saangi was kind of young to have that kind of responsibility, but then again, I was only fourteen when I became a Traveler. Still, Saangi seemed more like an eager kid than a future warrior who could help us defeat a world-crushing demon. But that's just me.

"Do not be upset, Saangi," Loor said, taking the edge off her voice. "You were concerned about me and for that I am grateful. But it would not look right for me to be quenching my thirst during a fight over water."

Saangi nodded. "I understand," she said. "But do not begin the battle until I get there!" She turned and ran back the way she had come.

"She is so young," Loor said as we watched her run away. "I wish she did not have to know of the danger we are all in."

"Hey, you and I aren't exactly ancient," I said. "I'd just as soon not know so much either."

Loor gave me a quick look, and continued walking.

"So what exactly is the point of this fight?" I asked, hurrying to keep up.

"It is a contest," Loor answered. "You have seen how precious water is in the city. The situation has become so desperate, it has turned us against one another."

"You mean the Batu against the Rokador?"

"It is worse than that," she answered. "Since the underground rivers have gone dry, the Batu are fighting among themselves in their quest for water. Families guard their small supplies fiercely. It is not uncommon for neighbors to battle one another over a small puddle after a rain shower."

One look around confirmed what Loor was saying. When I first saw Xhaxhu, the city was an amazing, fertile oasis in the middle of the desert. Troughs of fresh, clean water ran along the streets. There were rich palm trees, colorful hanging gardens and even fountains that sprayed water in intricate patterns around the massive statues of stone. But now, the city was dry. Bone dry. The troughs were empty, except for dust. The gardens were gone. The palm trees were dying. Sand from the desert blew through the streets and collected in every corner. Walking through Xhaxhu, I couldn't help but imagine that this is what the cities of ancient Egypt must have looked like when the desert began taking over. Unless something changed, I could imagine the city of Xhaxhu one day being buried in sand, waiting for some future civilization to uncover it.

Loor continued, "It has caused a divide among the Ghee warriors. Half of us remain loyal to our mission. We protect Xhaxhu and the royal family of Zinj."

"And the other half?" I asked.

"They have the same goal, but differ in their methods. The royal family has made it known that they wish to work through this catastrophe peacefully. But there is a growing number of Ghee warriors who feel our only hope of survival is to wage war on the Rokador below and claim whatever water they may be holding. With each passing day, the numbers of this rebellious group grow larger. If this drought continues, I fear their will be war."

"Smells like Saint Dane's kind of party," I said.

"I agree," Loor answered. "He has found a time in our history where we are the most vulnerable. The question is, what is he doing to make it worse?"

"That's always the question," I added. "Tell me about this fight we're going to."

"A well was discovered," Loor answered. "It is not known how much water it contains. It may hold a few feet, or lead to a spring. The dispute is over who will control it. The rebel Ghee warriors want it for themselves, to fortify their strength in preparation for their assault on the Rokador. The Ghee loyal to the royal family wish to put the well in the family's control, to distribute to all the people of Xhaxhu."

"So this is a battle between Ghee warriors?"

"It is," Loor answered somberly.

"Which side are you on?" I asked.

"I would like to believe I am on the side of Zadaa," Loor answered. "But in this case I am loyal to the royal family. I do not wish to see a war . . . for many reasons."

"I hear you," I said.

We traveled the rest of the way in silence. Loor needed to get her game on, and I needed to keep a low profile in case a thirsty Ghee warrior saw me and felt like beating up on a Rokador. Loor led me to a city square that was nothing more than a sandy patch of ground surrounded on all sides by towering, sandstone buildings. They reminded me of pictures I'd seen of ancient Mayan temples in Central America.

The buildings rose up like multi-tiered pyramids, finished off with flat tops. Some were taller than others, reaching maybe ten stories high. On all levels were carved statues that I can only guess were famous Batu from the past. Most of them looked like fierce warriors, clutching spears or arrows. It wasn't a real happy-looking bunch.

In the dead center of the square was an ornate fountain. Dry, of course. The fountain had a statue that was a larger-than-life depiction of a Ghee warrior battling a huge beast that looked like a fierce cat . . . with two heads. The beast stood on its hind legs, towering over the warrior with its claws out and ready to slice.

"That monster looks familiar," I said. "But that's impossible."

"It is not impossible because you have seen one before," Loor answered. "It is a zhou beast. That machine on Veelox took the image of the zhou from my memory and—"

"The Reality Bug!" I exclaimed. "I remember! When it burst out of Lifelight, it looked like that thing. You're saying those bad boys are real?"

Before Loor could answer, a trumpet sounded a fanfare. I looked up to see that people were gathering on the tiers of the pyramidlike buildings.

"How come nobody's on the ground?" I asked.

"Because that is the battleground," Loor answered.

"Oh," I said. "I guess I don't want to be here either."

"I would prefer you were nowhere near here," Loor said.

"But I want to see what happens," I said. "I'll be careful."

If she was scared, she didn't show it. After all we'd been through, I can't remember once when Loor was actually afraid. She was incredible. Or incredibly oblivious.

"So . . . , uh, win. Okay?" I said.

"I always do," she said with absolute confidence.

I didn't want to wish her luck because I felt like that would be bad luck. I know, that's dumb, but what can I say? I left Loor and found some stairs up to the first-balcony tier. Climbing the stairs wasn't fun. I had to make sure the dark cloak covered my head and arms. Sweat ran into my eyes, making them sting, but I had to keep it on. Man, it was hot. Did I mention that?

I found a secluded spot in the shade of a towering statue and took up my position to watch events unfold below. Looking down on the square, I got the feeling that we were in an arena. The tiers of the buildings around the square were filling up with spectators to complete the illusion. Either the people of Xhaxhu really cared about how this fight was going to play out, or they had nothing better to do with their time. Either way, there was a pretty decent turnout.

As I looked around at the gathering masses, trying to be invisible, I saw something strange. The more I thought about it, the more intrigued I became. Xhaxhu was crazy hot. I said that, right? All the people were dressed accordingly, wearing short, lightweight clothes. I saw several Ghee warriors who stood out in the crowd only because they were wearing black, light armor like Loor's. Everyone else was dressed for hanging out in a blast furnace except for me . . . and one other person.

One tier above me, keeping to the shadow of a statue, was someone else wearing a cloak over his head. I didn't think many people saw him because they were all looking down into the square. I may have been one of the few who actually was in a position to see him. Or her. I couldn't tell which, so I'll refer to him as "he." His cloak was dark, but not black. It looked more like a deep, deep purple. Whoever this mysterious guy was, there were two things I knew about him: One, he didn't want to be seen any more than I did; and two, he was very interested in the battle about to take place. Actually there was one other thing I knew. Unless he was some kind of freak, he had to be as hot as I was. But that only made his being there all the more interesting.

A trumpet fanfare sounded again, and the crowd grew quiet. From two different sides of the square, the contestants entered. Each group had three Ghee warriors who marched in together, their heads held high. Loor was one of them. She was also the only girl. It made me incredibly proud, and more than a little scared. More scary was the fact that they all carried weapons. I had seen war games here on Zadaa a while back. In that battle the contestants used short wooden sticks to knock colored pegs off their opponents. It was more like a brutal game of capture the flag than real war. Not this time. Here in the dry, dusty square, each warrior had a small shield in one hand, and a short, sharp sword in the other.

Sharp swords meant blood. My heart raced. This was no game.

The two groups of warriors met near the fountain in the center of the square, saluted each other with their swords and stepped back. The crowd cheered its approval. Another Ghee warrior entered the square. He strode to the center and stood between the two trios of warriors. He saluted Loor's group, then the other. He looked up at the crowd and announced: "The challenge has been set. The stakes are clear."

I half expected the guy to shout: "Leeeeet's get ready to rummmmble!" He didn't.

He continued, "To the victor goes the right to control the newly discovered well. The match will follow in the long tradition of the Ghee. Victory shall go to the warrior who cleanly severs two heads."

The crowd cheered. My knees went weak. Did I hear right? Were these guys going to go after one another's heads?

I wanted to scream. I wanted to jump down, grab Loor, and pull her out of there. This was insane! I felt totally, absolutely helpless. As impossible as this sounds, I started to sweat some more.

The Ghee announcer shouted, "To the brave, we salute you!"

He saluted the first trio, then Loor and her team. The crowd cheered again. My stomach twisted. There was every possibility that in a few minutes, Loor would be dead. And for what? A drink of water? The announcer walked quickly out of the killing box. Once he was clear, the two groups of warriors faced each other, and saluted again with their swords.

I wanted to shout out, "Stop!" but that would have been about as stupid as this whole spectacle. The two trios of warriors backed off from each other, while keeping their eyes on their opponents. The crowd quieted. It was eerie. There must have been a thousand people lining the balconies of that square, but for that one moment, all I could hear was the wind from the desert blowing through the arid streets of Xhaxhu.

The trumpet sounded again. The battle was on.

ZADAA

The two trios of warriors faced off against each other in the dry, dusty square. They all looked pretty scary, wearing the black leather armor of the Ghee. They were definitely pros . . . all muscle with short lethal swords and cold eyes fixed on their opponents. I saw no difference between the group loyal to the royal family of Xhaxhu, and the rebels who wanted to start a war with the Rokador. They all just looked like . . . warriors. And Loor's being the only girl among them didn't mean she was at a disadvantage. No way. I'd seen her level guys who towered over her. But when you had six fierce warriors mixing it up with swords, anything could happen.

I stole a quick glance up to the mysterious guy who was watching from above. He was hidden beneath his purple cloak, so I couldn't get a good look at his face. I wondered if he was a Rokador trying to blend in, like I was. Seeing him stand there made me realize that wearing a heavy cloak in this kind of heat probably made us stand out more than if we were walking around with our white skin gleaming in the sun. The truth was, it didn't matter. Nobody cared about us. All eyes were focused down into the square, waiting for the carnage.

The warriors didn't move. I wondered if there was going to be some kind of signal to start the fight. Would there be a whistle? Was a referee going to come in and drops his hand? Or maybe this was more like a quick draw, where the action would begin as soon as somebody twitched. My stomach turned at the thought that I would see these warriors going at it until two of their heads were lopped off. I never even thought I could stomach one of those bullfights where the poor bull was skewered at the end. That was bad enough. The idea of people being decapitated went way past gross and into the land of gruesome. Even worse, the idea that one of them was Loor made me go numb. It was like a dream. A really bad dream.

The two groups stood that way for what seemed like forever. I was dying. When was this going to start? The answer came a moment later. What happened wasn't at all what I expected. In some ways, it was worse.

The silence was torn by a hideous sound such as I had never heard before. It was like an angry screech that came from some vicious animal. In fact, that's exactly what it was. A gasp went up from the crowd when two doors were flung open at the base of one of the buildings, and a black zhou beast charged into the square.

Yikes.

The danger just got dialed up. The beast looked pretty much like the statue in the center of the square. It was a giant cat, way bigger than the klees of Eelong, which were pretty much human-size. If it was up on its hind legs, this thing would be taller than Loor by five feet. Its paws were immense, with six curved claws—I could tell because those lethal claws were out and ready for action. The beast was mostly black, but its fur had shiny spots of red blood oozing from small wounds everywhere. I guessed that somebody must have stabbed at it a bunch of times so it would be PO'd enough to fight, like with a bullfight. It was a logical guess, because this monster definitely wanted a piece of somebody. It leaped from the open doorway, ready to roll. Instantly the door was slammed shut behind it. Whoever was inside didn't want this bad boy to turn around and jump back in, looking for the guy who punched it full of holes. The monster crouched on all fours, looking around for something to chew. It snarled viciously revealing razorlike fangs. My mouth went dry.

Oh yeah, in case you forgot, the zhou beast had two heads, both with equally long, sharp fangs. The two heads acted separately, peering around with keen eyes. I wondered which head was the one that controlled the rest of the body. If one wanted to go right and the other left, well, that would be interesting. This whole event would have been interesting, if Loor hadn't been down there about to be eaten.

The two teams of warriors went into action. They held their swords and shields out defensively. I quickly realized that they weren't interested in fighting one another. This was all about the zhou beast. Two heads had to be severed. That's what the announcer had said. I had to guess that the two heads he was talking about belonged to the zhou thingy. The contest was really about which team would get the heads. At first I was relieved that Loor wasn't in danger of being killed by a fellow Ghee. But it was quickly replaced by the fear she would be killed by a two-headed cat monster. Dead is dead.

The two trios of warriors circled the beast. The monster whipped its heads back and forth, watching them. After a few seconds of this size-up, the beast stopped snarling and crouched low, its tail whipping back and forth like, well, like an angry cat. I wasn't sure if it was afraid, or surrendering, or getting ready to spring.

Loor's team struck first. One warrior had a rope and lassoed the zhou like a rodeo cowboy, snaring one of its heads. The crowd roared its approval. But before Loor or her other teammate could make the next move, the rival team took advantage. One of the warriors leaped on to the back of the zhou and raised his sword, ready to plunge it into the back of the two-headed cat. Bad move. Only one of the zhou's heads was being controlled by Loor's teammate. The other head was free and looking for trouble. Before the warrior could attack, the zhou's free head twisted around at an angle that I didn't think was possible. I guess the warrior on its back didn't think it was possible either, or he wouldn't have been dumb enough to be there. The zhou clamped its mouth around the legs of its tormentor, making the warrior scream in agony. He was so surprised that he didn't even use his sword. The zhou yanked the warrior off its back and started snapping its head back and forth . . . with the warrior's leg still in its mouth, the owner along for the ride.

It was gruesome to see this guy being whipped around like a toy, but I didn't want to miss anything, so I sort of squinted. I know, what a wuss, but my words can't describe how horrible it was. After a few seconds the zhou spit the warrior out, sending him crashing down to the dusty ground. His armor was torn and there was blood everywhere, but he was alive. Loor and her team grabbed the rope and worked together to pull the zhou away from the fallen warrior. The zhou fought back, but Loor and the others managed to drag it far enough away from the injured warrior so that his teammates could run in to rescue him. I thought that was a pretty good show of sportsmanship. They had saved their opponent's life.

As it turned out, the injured guy's teammates weren't as caring as Loor's team. Nobody went to his rescue. They let him lie there, dying. I didn't know which was worse, seeing this guy nearly bitten in half, or knowing that his friends didn't care about saving his life. That told me a lot about the Ghee warriors who favored war against the Rokador. They were cold-blooded . . . just the kind of guys Saint Dane loves to hang with. Note to self: Keep an eye on the rebel Ghee warriors.

Things got worse. The zhou suddenly sprang into the air so quickly that the crowd gasped. I did too. This beast got some serious vertical. It moved so quickly that it took Loor's team by surprise. It yanked the rope away from Loor and one other warrior. The third warrior wasn't so lucky. He got his arm wrapped up in the rope. The zhou whipped its head back, pulling the helpless warrior off his feet. The zhou's next move was to pounce on the fallen Ghee. The poor guy tried to roll away, but he was so tangled in his own rope he couldn't move fast enough. Unlike Loor's team, the rival warriors weren't about to try and save him either. No big surprise.

But Loor tried. Without hesitation she leaped at the zhou, shield first. With one arm she slammed her shield into one head, while slashing at the other with her sword. Both heads reared back in surprise and pain, which gave Loor the time she needed. With one continuous move she spun back, slashing her sword again, severing the rope that tied her fallen friend to the zhou. Their other teammate was able to pull the guy to his feet and get him away before the zhou could come after them again.

Round one went to the zhou beast. Round two went to Loor. But the beast didn't look any worse for the wear, and both Ghee teams were hurting. I wondered what would happen if there was no way they could slay this thing. How would this end? Was this going to be a fight to the death for both sides?

~ PENDRAGON ~

The next move was the beast's. Loor had hurt him. She had drawn blood. He was ticked. He wanted revenge.

He went after Loor.

Before she realized that she was being attacked, the beast lashed out at her arm, slashing her shoulder. Loor dove away, and dropped her sword. This was bad. All she had left to protect herself was the lame little shield. The beast kept after her. Loor needed help.

"The rope," she ordered her teammates as she rolled away from the two-headed cat. Her team went after the rope as she jumped up and bolted in the other direction. The zhou wasn't fooled. He was right after her. Loor sprinted toward the fallen warrior from the other team. What was she doing? The big zhou leaped into the air. Loor dove to the ground, tucked, rolled, and grabbed the sword from the injured warrior's hand. Yes! She was armed again! The zhou landed, ready to attack. Loor quickly slashed at its front paws. The beast screamed in pain and fell hard, headfirst. Or, headsfirst. Faceplant into the dirt. Or facesplant.

Loor rolled away, having dodged death once again. But the zhou wasn't finished. Not by far. Loor jumped to her feet, and was headed back to her teammates when one of the rival warriors tackled her. I couldn't believe it! She never saw him coming. The crowd booed, but it didn't stop the warrior. He yanked the sword away from her. I guess he felt it belonged to his team, but c'mon! Before Loor had a chance to react, the rival warrior was scampering back to join his own teammate. I was beginning to hate these guys. Loor was once again without a weapon.

The zhou was getting back to his feet. Loor's teammates were on the other side of the square, holding the rope, ready to help. She wasn't even close to them. She was on her own. The zhou got its wits back, scanned the square with both heads, and spotted Loor. She was out in the open, totally defenseless. The zhou squatted down like a cat ready to pounce. I thought there was nowhere for Loor to go. But I was wrong. Before the beast leaped, Loor sprinted for the center of the square and the statue in the dry fountain.

"Run!" I shouted, like she needed to be reminded.

She made it to the statue of the Ghee warrior battling the zhou and climbed. The crowd was going nuts. Loor had become the favorite. I had no idea what she was going to do up there, except maybe buy a little time. I sure hoped the zhou couldn't climb. If it could, Loor would be trapped, and finished. Her teammates didn't know what to do, and the rival team certainly wasn't going to bail her out. She was climbing up onto a dead end. Dead being the operative word.

She had gotten part way up the statue when I saw someone sprinting across the square. At first I thought it was one of the other warriors, but a quick look showed me that someone else had entered the contest. It was Saangi, Loor's squire. What was she doing? She definitely had a plan, because her head was down and her legs were pumping. She didn't have a weapon, and even if she did, I didn't think she stood a chance against the zhou. One thing was sure. This young girl had guts.

On the other side of the statue, the zhou was crouched and stalking. Either it didn't feel like there was any need to rush, or its paws were too slashed up to run. Whatever. It was closing in on Loor. Whatever Saangi had planned, she had to do it fast. She ran to the spot where Loor had dropped her sword, and scooped it up. Without hesitating, she turned and sprinted for the statue.

"Loor!" she shouted, and threw the sword.

Loor looked in time to see her sword sailing toward her. For a brief second my heart stopped, thinking Loor was about to be impaled by her own sword. I should have known better. Loor plucked the sword out of the air like a pro because, well, she was a pro. I guess Saangi wasn't so bad either. But this impressive move alone wasn't going to win the battle.

The zhou had decided to throw away caution. It began to charge. The final attack was on. Loor was about to reach the highest point of the statue, which was on top of the zhou heads. There was some kind of symbolism here that I didn't bother to analyze. It was pretty clear to me that this statue wasn't tall enough. If the zhou could still jump half as high as I'd seen before, he would nail Loor, sword or not.

But Loor's teammates didn't let her down. Before the big cat made its final leap, they tossed the rope at it, lassoing its leg. The beast's eyes were intent on Loor and didn't see it coming. The two warriors yanked hard, keeping the zhou from leaping. The surprised beast looked down at the rope . . .

And Loor made her move.

She leaped off the statue and onto the back of the zhou. But unlike the rival warrior who had tried this before, Loor's weapon was ready. I think the sword hit its mark before Loor's feet hit its back. The power of her fall drove the sword deep into the back of the zhou, all the way to the handle. It was horrible and strange to see both heads react with surprise and agony. Its body arched up so quickly, it threw Loor off. She landed hard, rolled, then popped up, ready to finish the job.

She was too late. No sooner had she been thrown, than the two rival warriors leaped onto the back of the wounded zhou. Using their swords, they slashed at its dying heads. This time I had to look away. No way I wanted to see this. Luckily the crowd was in an uproar, so I didn't have to hear it either. Half the crowd was cheering because the battle was won, the other half was booing because the true winner,

Loor, was not going to come away with the prize. This was all about who got the heads. Loor and her team may have stopped the zhou, but they did not get the heads. A technicality, but those were the rules. I didn't think it was fair, but I was more relieved that Loor had survived.

I stood with my back to the square, not wanting to imagine how gruesome the scene was on the ground. As I stood there, I glanced up to the next level to see how the strange observer with the purple robe was reacting. Whose side was he on? Would he be cheering, or jeering?

I never found out, because he was gone.

Award-winning Fantasy from
NANCY FARMER

THE FARSALA TRILOGY CONTINUES

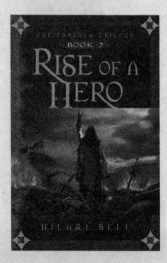

MORE FULL-BLOODED FANTASY FROM SIMON & SCHUSTER

Which ones have you read?

THE RETURN OF TAMORA PIERCE'S BELOVED QUARTETS

The Immortals
- ☐ Wild Magic
- ☐ Wolf-speaker
- ☐ Emperor Mage
- ☐ The Realms of the Gods

Song of the Lioness
- ☐ Alanna: The First Adventure
- ☐ In the Hand of the Goddess
- ☐ The Woman Who Rides Like a Man
- ☐ Lioness Rampant

KEN OPPEL'S ACCLAIMED FANTASY ADVENTURE TRILOGY

The Silverwing Sequence
- ☐ Silverwing
- ☐ Sunwing
- ☐ Firewing

SUSAN COOPER'S AWARD-WINNING FANTASY SERIES

The Dark Is Rising Sequence
- ☐ Over Sea, Under Stone
- ☐ The Dark Is Rising
- ☐ Greenwitch
- ☐ The Grey King
- ☐ Silver on the Tree

The magic continues
with more fantasies from
Aladdin Paperbacks